Short fiction available from The Ecco Press:

Ellen Hunnicutt

In the Music Library

Winner of the Drue Heinz Literature Prize 1987

THE ECCO PRESS
NEW YORK

First published in 1988 by The Ecco Press
26 West 17th Street, New York, NY 10011
Published simultaneously in Canada by
Penguin Books Canada Ltd., Ontario
Printed in the United States of America

This edition in arrangement with the University of Pittsburgh Press

"At St. Theresa's College for Women" first appeared in the *Cimarron Review* and is reprinted here with the permission of the Board of Regents for Oklahoma State University, holders of the copyright. "There Is a Balm in Gilead" originally appeared in *Mississippi Review*, "All Kinds of Flowers" is reprinted from *Indiana Review*, "Energy" was first published in *Michigan Quarterly Review*, and "In the Music Library" and "When I Was Married" were originally published in *Prairie Schooner*.

Library of Congress Cataloging-in-Publication Data

Hunnicutt, Ellen.
In the music library.
"Winner of the Drue Heinz Literature Prize, 1987"
Contents: At St. Theresa's College for Women
There is a balm in Gilead
All kinds of flowers
[etc.]
I. Title.
PS3558.U466515   1988   813'.54   87-20061

ISBN 0-88001-210-2

for Zerl

Contents

In the Music Library

At St. Theresa's College for Women

"I don't know who tunes the fiddles," says Sister Theophane. "Fourteen?" I am only half listening.

"'They play the Bach Double Concerto but I don't think they can tune their own violins.'" She reads this information from a letter, refolds the page, looks into her coffee cup and finds it empty. One more betrayal.

"Perhaps they never go out of tune," I offer. "The Japanese can do anything these days." I am thinking about gardenias, my very first corsage, how my fingers ached to touch the soft ivory petals. *Any place you touch will turn brown.* This is my mother's voice. The fretful, rising tone is perfectly preserved in my memory, like the fingering pattern for an extended arpeggio that, once learned, lives on forever in the brain cells. "What ever happened to gardenias?" I ask Sister Theophane.

"Opal, please be serious. Success depends on seeing to details. I've spent half my budget on these children, half the budget for the entire series."

"I'll help you tune," I say, contrite. "What's fourteen fiddles? Even if you are putting me out of business."

Sister Theophane rises, takes both our cups for more coffee, hers in the left hand (sugar), mine in the right (black). "You have tenure, Opal." A gentle reprimand.

In the cafeteria at St. Theresa's College for Women, at four in the afternoon, it is 1949. I am eighteen and nothing has happened yet. It is a trick of the light, pale Chicago sun slanting through the high iron fence, bathing our simple buildings

3

in a certain yellow glow that is inexpressibly sad. In many ways, St. Theresa's exists outside of time; many things have not changed since I was a student here. That is because nuns never wear anything out; and at St. Theresa's nobody vandalizes. Unscarred maple floor, golden oak dining tables, cool pink marble windowsills and, beyond the windows, the small sandstone chapel.

But I am not eighteen, and Sister Theophane in a neat blue dress, professor of music and my boss, thick-waisted and graying above the coffee cups is actually two years younger than I.

"I've decided to offer them ice cream," Theophane says, heartened by fresh coffee. "Lemonade might make them need the bathroom."

"They'll probably need the bathroom anyway."

"Opal, will you please stop it? You aren't helping. You really aren't."

"I'm sorry. I've just turned fifty. It's made me touchy."

Theophane considers, decides to say nothing, opens and reads again the letter from her friend, a nun in Indianapolis.

Why are joy and sadness so inextricably mixed? Memory and desire. I have a third-year student who is setting parts of *The Waste Land* to music for women's choir. She rehearses her singers in a basement room where someone is growing an ivy philodendron on a high windowsill. I listen to the voices, study the deep green of leaves spilling over the cool basement wall, and it seems to me there is some important thing I need to know, hidden in the voices of these young women.

One day last week I drove home by St. Luke's Hospital where nuns still wear habits. I paid a dollar to a parking attendant and sat quietly in the lobby of the hospital for an hour, to watch the nuns. This recalled for me, oddly, not my childhood among teaching sisters but nuns in old films, moving across the landscape of faraway countries bringing succor to the needy. I saw a priest who looked like actor Barry Fitzgerald.

An hour later, moving through the glut of Chicago traffic, this experience lost all reality for me. I wondered if I had, indeed, been at St. Luke's. Sometimes this happens to me when I am teaching. I fancy a student will suddenly look at me and discover I am not a teacher at all, but an uncertain young woman like herself, masquerading in a middle-aged body. The two things are not precisely the same.

"Fifty," I say in the dark, moving close to Howie.

"I'm glad you're not fat," he says against my throat. It is the lopsided compliment too-thin women receive all of their lives. "Jack Webster's wife must be three feet across in the butt." He strokes my skinny butt gratefully.

"Howie, I need to know something."

"Okay."

"Do you think about girls? I want you to tell me."

"All the time," he answers promptly. "That's all I think about, naked girls standing in long lines, day and night."

"Please, I want to know. I'm not young anymore."

"Neither am I," says Howie, refusing to play games.

I do this to him almost daily, compulsively.

Theophane, my closest friend, is silent across the table. I wonder what her fantasies are, what nuns dream about.

Howie is an engineer, of the old school: get the work out. Georgia Tech, class of '51. He does not spend time planning utopias as many of the younger men do. Such things may come. Howie has no objection. But he isn't counting on it.

He flies to Boston (often) to supervise the installation of packaging machinery. In his pockets and in the expensive briefcase I gave him for Christmas he carries calipers, socket wrenches, locking pliers, a set of screwdrivers. Traveling, he is

5

a walking hardware store. When he goes through airport security, he buzzes. Howie always buzzes. In an illogical, ridiculous way this pleases me. I'm glad I am married to a man who buzzes in airport security.

"Bring me something from Boston," I say petulantly.

Howie dutifully complies. At the end of the week he returns, bringing me two rolls of Lifesavers and a coffee mug. You can't shop in airports.

I thank him with a thin smile, set the mug on a kitchen shelf, serve dinner with cool, elaborate gestures, making it clear that I have been wounded.

At four in the morning I wake suddenly, gripped with remorse, gut-wrenching terror. Howie sleeping peacefully beside me is fifty-four, could die at any time. He has passed the age where people say, "What a tragedy, so young." They would say, "Howard Franklin? What did he have?" I slip from bed in the darkness, go to a hall closet and dig out the old air force jacket Howie wore in college, bury my face in it and weep piteously, seeing my husband in his grave and wondering what I should do with the second car. I have never learned to make out an automobile title. I determine to learn at once. This small decision calms me and I am glad Howie has not heard nor seen me. My hands release the jacket and I picture this calm, capable woman I have become: giving directions, signing papers, saying, "What, after all, is death? A change in mode from major to minor, a shift in tempo, a variation on a theme." All of our children are dead. Why not Howie? Why not me? Such things are easy. That's it, isn't it?

My mother never understood why all of our babies died. One two three four five. Like little Indians.

"Darling, people have one miscarriage," she said, visiting me at the hospital. "Everyone has one miscarriage. It's common." Somehow this was meant as instruction, like telling me to whip the fudge just until it loses its glossy sheen.

I swam up from a fuzzy sea of contradictions and drugs—

scopolamine in those days—and pressed my fingertips against the outline of my uterus, a curious, swollen mass lying just beneath the skin of my abdomen. Then, for the one and only time in my life, I had a vision. I saw my mother going through supermarkets and department stores, making her private survey, stopping women with plump babies and curly-headed toddlers. All of them told her they had, indeed, had one miscarriage, between babies, probably a deformed fetus and all for the good. And mother, nodding, made check marks on a piece of paper that looked like a birth announcement. Scopolamine works on the mind.

Mother twisted her handkerchief, displayed courage, was admirable. Then bitter, shivery little sobs forced themselves from her throat. Against her will, she cried. Pushed past her limit, by me. Life until that time had been a trick done with mirrors; then the mirrors were snatched away.

This memory is self-serving. I savor the delicious tang of betrayal like rich dessert across my tongue, pity poor Theophane who has not suffered as I have, feel generous toward her because of this.

What, after all, is death? I know death the way I know a student composition. "Wait until you hear it!" cries the eager student. But I hear it already, just looking at the score. Epistemology of music notation.

After the fifth and final miscarriage, Howie and I lay side by side in the darkness, numb and shaken. "It's going to be all right," he said protectively, but with a hostile edge to his voice. Someone was to blame. Soon he would find the target for his anger. Any minute now. But he never did. Howie never got revenge. What he got was a promotion.

I got Robert, eleven years old, near-sighted. "Mrs. Franklin?" Robert's mother was an eager, huffy little voice in the telephone. "I understand you used to play violin with the symphony." When excited, she talked through her nose.

7

"I don't play any more. I don't teach."

"Robert isn't doing at all well in the class at school. We want private lessons for him with a skilled person." She came down hard on "skilled." Had she already interviewed and rejected a dozen teachers? Robert's mother was formidable. She did all of the right things for the wrong reasons, knew that any violinist who refused to teach her son had to be good. Damned good. "Don't give me an answer today, Mrs. Franklin." Robert's mother eventually found her true vocation, now sells insurance.

"Vibrate slowly," I said to Robert, "like an owl. Who-uh, who-uh, who-uh. After you smooth out the wiggle-waggle, you can speed up." Nobody had ever said this to Robert before and he didn't mind trying it. He was fascinated with a teacher who wore velvet pants and chain-smoked through the lesson.

"Can I ride in your Porsche?" he asked. At the end of the lesson, his mother handed me a five-dollar bill.

That night at dinner I showed the money to Howie. "I can buy my own cigarettes." He grinned, then he got up and put brandy in the coffee. I carried the bill folded in my wallet all week, and walked through shops looking at things that cost five dollars.

Incredibly, Robert liked me. He brought me sticks of Dentyne gum and told me jokes.

"To read a signature in sharps," I said to him "look at the last sharp on the right and go up one."

"Jesus, that's a neat trick," said Robert, who was just learning to swear.

I laid plans to steal Robert and flee to Australia. I'd call Howie from Brisbane and make him understand. Or maybe Canada. Howie could commute while the litigation dragged out.

Robert, who was ordinary, brought in his wake Clarissa, who was exceptional. Plain, stout, brilliant. Eyes as cool and clever as a leopard's. She was fifteen, and she hated me. Her vibrato was pure, no wiggle-waggle, and she knew it. She knew everything.

"All music imitates the human voice," I told her.

"I know that," said Clarissa.

"Sing the music as you play. When you're able to do that, you can just breathe with it. The length of one breath is the basis for all phrasing."

"I know that," said Clarissa, a reflex. She was an inch taller than I with powerful arms and hands and the perfect apple skin that plump little girls often carry into adolescence. When she is forty, I thought, she will be a handsome woman. She reminded me of pictures I had seen of Anna Freud. Except for the hatred in her face.

But she came back week after week, often with her lesson memorized. "Your instincts are good," I said to her. "Trust them. When the wispy little business starts in your head, don't cut it off. Nurture it." Her attack was masterly, a thick, brown bite, slightly bitter, understated, theatrical.

I wanted to steal her, run away to Argentina. "You'll like Buenos Aires," I'd say, and Clarissa would answer, "I know that."

I received the first phone call from her grandfather. Elderly, Russian-born, he called Leningrad St. Petersburg. He loved the violin the way some men love beautiful women. "The child sounds better. Thank you."

"She's doing it herself." Which was true.

"I am now prepared to buy her a better instrument." He named the amount he was willing to spend.

It caught me off guard. "You can't be serious." I stammered, gushed, sounded ridiculous. "For that money you could have a Guarnerius."

A Guarnerius, it seemed, was exactly what he had in mind. "What if she stops practicing?" I asked.

He chuckled. "She won't, and a fiddle is always an investment. I can't lose." Although he did not play himself, he had already owned a Stradivarius, sold it, now missed it. "I'd rather pay the finder's fee to you, Mrs. Franklin. You know the child best."

"Me," I told Howie.

"You can do it," he said. "Why not?"

"When he sees me he'll change his mind."

But the grandfather came over the following evening, shook my hand, and seemed satisfied. He smoked a cigar and drank Scotch with Howie. As a young student in Germany he had met Clara Schumann, heard her tell the wonderful stories about Brahms. I put it together—Clara, Clarissa. "Mrs. Franklin," he said, "Clarissa is modeling herself after you. She has purchased a pair of shoes exactly like the ones you are wearing."

"Clarissa?" It was news to me.

That night I dreamed I telephoned Clara Schumann and asked her to find a fiddle. She was barefoot, offered to trade a fiddle for a pair of shoes. In the dream I spoke fluent German, a language I do not know.

Actually, I called Altman, my own former teacher, retired in San Diego. "Opal!" he cried. "Bring Howie and come to California. We'll eat clams, just like the old days in Chicago. My wife died. Did you know that?" Altman said, "Zenger's the best. In Cleveland. You call Zenger." Zenger said he'd talk to St. Louis and get back to me.

Clarissa's Guarnerius was in Amsterdam. A rich, winey beauty. With it, she caught fire, plunged into Paganini, Sarasate, Saint-Saëns, Wieniawski. I had to call Altman again. "She needs a teacher. She plays better than I do."

"Listen, Opal," said Altman, "I can get you into a quartet out here. It's hard today, very hard. The kids coming on are good. They show up knowing all the standard repertoire already. But I can get you in." He wanted to hear Clarissa play.

"On the telephone?"

"Yes."

But the grandfather found out and didn't like it. He bought airline tickets and sent Clarissa and me to California.

Flying terrified Clarissa. She clutched her fiddle case, fought nausea, turned white, bit her lips. And finally surrendered. "Mrs. Franklin, do you know why I hate you so much?" Her voice was a gray wisp, devoid of hope.

"Yes," I said. Gently, oh so gently. "Because I'm thin . . . and you think thin is beautiful."

Then her tears came, and small, bitter sobs. "I want to change. You'll help me . . . I know you will."

"Like hell I will," I said, capturing her in my arms. "You're a wonderful, marvelous person, just as you are." So I told her about the babies. I told her about Brisbane and Buenos Aires. I even told her about my mother and scopolamine.

"So nobody gets everything," said Clarissa, sniffling.

We landed, not healed, but holding hands. Eight years later, while on tour, Clarissa sent me a postcard from Buenos Aires: "Hey, I'm here! Come on down! Love always, Clarissa."

Altman said, "Juilliard."

"That's what I thought," I said, but the grandfather paid for everything and seemed pleased.

He met our return plane. "She'll need a high school equivalency," I told him.

"We'll get a tutor," he said. "Go ahead with her preparation."

When I got Clarissa past her auditions, the grandfather appeared at my door with roses and kissed my hand.

After Clarissa came Dwight, Stephen, Mary Ruth, Annette. Twin brothers who went into country music and still send me chocolates at Christmas. A quiet boy who loved Debussy and became a Lutheran minister. A gentle girl with white hands who, incredibly, committed suicide. More names than I can remember. But never another Clarissa.

In the same month, Altman died and St. Theresa's offered

me a job. I received a call from Sister Mary Elizabeth. "Mrs. Franklin? Sister Theophane wants you for our music department." Mary Elizabeth is nothing like her fragile name. President of St. Theresa's, one hundred pounds of intensity, tough, formidable fund-raiser, frequenter of Chicago boardrooms.

"Sister, I'm afraid I'm not a very good Catholic."

"Who is these days? I wasn't proposing to hire you as a theologian. We already have a couple of those. We're looking for a violin teacher. You graduated from St. Theresa's, also studied privately, and played professionally. That combination makes you interesting to us. Come in and we'll talk about it."

"All right. Has everything changed?"

"Yes and no."

Sister Mary Elizabeth, wearing a gabardine suit, received me in her small, pleasant rooms: sliced cheese, poured cider. "We're putting together a music performance major. We've never offered it before. We've turned out school teachers, nurses, and secretaries."

"I can't imagine St. Theresa's changing. It looks the same."

"Read Father Newman, unfolding revelation. Our mission is to educate women. On any two successive days that means two different things, at least two."

"Ah!" Sister Theophane came in and settled into a chair. "If you're going to cite Father Newman then cite Prometheus as well."

Mary Elizabeth smiled. "Sister means we've been criticized, but that's nothing new. There's always been something a little illicit about educating people, especially women. For years our simplicity was protective coloration—cloisters, high walls, habits—to cover what we were really doing."

"Commiting a crime?" Theophane asked cheerfully. "The first women composers were nuns. The orders sheltered them. And in the Middle Ages if you were fleeing an enemy you could run into a convent and claim sanctuary. And many

12

people did. It's never been strawberries and cream, keeping the flame and all that."

And so the sisters took me in, and now I have that commodity above price: a place to get up in the morning and go to.

"Opal?"

"I'm sorry, Sister. What did you say?"

"I asked if you were going to eat dinner with me tonight."

"No, I'm going home to eat. Look, you've managed St. Theresa's Fine Arts Series for nine years, three programs a year, almost without a flaw. I really think everything will be all right."

Theophane is not convinced. "I think I'll close up my office and see you in the morning."

"And I'd better call my husband."

"Howie?"

"Hi."

"I'll be here another hour."

"No problem."

"Sister Theophane's upset. She's afraid the Suzuki kids will play out of tune."

Howie likes Theophane, immediately takes sides. "Do you believe this guy really has fourteen prodigies?"

"Suzuki? He claims they aren't prodigies, just ordinary children taught by his method."

"Baloney," says Howie loyally. "Does Suzuki come with them?"

"No, he's too old to travel. He sends his assistant. Guess what the assistant's name is."

"What?"

"Honda."

"You made that up."

At the far end of the cafeteria the serving line opens and the first boarding students drift in. At St. Theresa's the median age of students used to be nineteen. Today it is twenty-six. The numbers are weighted by part-time students, day students, evening students. Our oldest student is a woman of seventy-one who is studying art history.

"Opal, you're still here!" Winifred Orbison in blue jeans brings her brown bag dinner to my table. Thirty-seven, mother of two, political science major, she does not have time for music. "I can't get one damned person to picket O'Hare Saturday afternoon."

"O'Hare?"

"A military air show. I can usually count on at least ten people, but everybody's going to hear those Japanese kids play. Opal, I don't mean to be rude but what the hell is your music going to be worth if they drop the bombs?" She eats her sandwich without tasting it. "Try a cookie. My daughter made them. She's twelve."

"Delicious! Tell her I said so."

"She cooks all the time, even bakes bread. She's four times smarter than I ever was. You should hear her father brag about her. Opal, the bombs scare the hell out of me. I tell people just to walk down that hall and look in the day nursery, just look in at those children and think about it. Have you ever done that?"

"Yes."

"I have to run."

Our day nursery is under the direction of Sister Angela. She is small and rosy with fluttering hands. She never tires of children. She wears a black tunic and slacks, sits on the carpet with small boys and girls while their mothers study. She charges one dollar an hour and insists on being paid promptly.

My last student cannot come in until after work, tonight

14

has been asked to work overtime. Betty. Bluff, bright, eager, she just wants to see if she can learn to play the violin. Last year she took a course in auto mechanics at the vocational school to see if she could learn to fix her own car. Betty has no sense of magic. "Count," I say to her. "Three-four time is a waltz. Do you dance?"

"Not the waltz."

I assign Beethoven's "Ode to Joy" in a student transcription, asking the music to do my job for me. "Five simple notes created the most glorious anthem the world has ever known."

"Can't I play a woman composer?"

"Yes . . . of course."

Cecile Chaminade's "Pas des Echarpes." She plays it mechanically, taking great care with the chromatics, as she takes great care with everything. I have four Bettys this year. The number is down slightly from last year.

The pleasant aromas of food drift through the room. Hannah passes. "Hi, Mrs. Franklin." A senior art student, she is graduating and being married in June. She has selected a china pattern, named her bridesmaids, asked me to play at her wedding.

"Hello, Mrs. Franklin." Marla is in music education. With her pleasant soprano voice she will teach school children to sing. Her parents' divorce has left her skittish about boys. She budgets her money carefully, sews her own clothes.

"Staying for dinner tonight, Mrs. Franklin?" Carol is twenty-two, an unmarried mother. Her parents care for her little boy while she studies nursing.

They come together, a line of bright flowers, all the modes of a scale, unique and yet related in an important and special way. They are the women I have always known, eager to laugh, nearly as eager to cry, filled with swift enthusiasm, sharp sorrow, enormous hope.

I rise, pass through the double doors, and bump squarely into Sister Theophane who is now smiling. "I read through everything again. Three teachers travel with them. They tune. Apparently my friend didn't know that."

"They don't need us, Sister. We're obsolete."

Theophane sighs. "I think you're teasing, but I will be so very glad when you get over this fifty business."

"Enjoy your dinner, Sister."

In the silent hallway my footsteps echo as in a cathedral, past deserted classrooms to my teaching studio. I think ahead to dinner, stopping on the way home for shrimp, Howie's favorite. At the doorway of the nursery I pause and look in at pale sunlight falling across soft carpeting, abandoned toys returned to bright shelves, silent walls. Five plush animals sit neatly on a windowsill: two bears, a rabbit, one soft cat, a perky dog. Misshapen from much hugging, inexpressibly sad. It is a trick of the light, the pale Chicago light that will be gone in a moment.

"Mrs. Franklin! I'm so sorry I'm late. Are you coming?"

"Yes. Yes, I'm coming."

There Is a Balm in Gilead

At the International House of Pancakes, where I have
breakfast most mornings, I often see a man who looks
like violinist Jascha Heifetz. He wears a yellow T-shirt, talks to
no one, crosses his arms and sweeps the room with cold gray
eyes. His resemblance to Heifetz is not a mere coincidence of
facial features (high brow, widely spaced eyes, gaunt cheeks),
it is mannerism as well, as if he has posed before a mirror for
a long time, practicing every gesture and expression in order
to carry out a meticulous impersonation, as if he has chosen
the yellow T-shirt after long deliberation. He is poised, remote
and regal. Sometimes I think I would like to write a note and
pass it along the counter to him: "My name is Emma, and I
know who you really are. There is an important question I
must ask you." But I do not know what the question is, nor
why it is important.

"Here is a paper, miss," says the black busboy. "This morning there are two house papers and two others that people
left behind."

"Thank you. That's a lot of papers."

"Yes, miss, a lot."

The busboy's only name appears to be Junior. This name is
embroidered on his shirt and he responds to it with a level,
untroubled expression. If it is a slur, he has been hearing it for
so long he has forgotten its origins, but perhaps it is not a
slur. Perhaps the name was given to him with a great deal of
love and care, and he has abstracted the sound of it from all

other sounds, now carries this sound about with him, just at the edge of consciousness. He moves confidently, arranges the scattered sheets of newspaper into orderly units. Junior understands the principle of organization.

GRADUATE RECORD EXAMINATIONS (GRE)
SUBJECT: Music
(Use number two lead pencil. If you do not have a pencil you may raise your hand and ask the monitor for one.)

1. What is the principle of organization in the following list of composers: Henk Badings, Alban Berg, Charles Ives, Igor Stravinsky

   a. All were German-born.
   b. All composed in the twentieth-century idiom.
   c. All drew their inspiration from religious sources.

"Over easy?" asks my waitress, a young woman who likes to do her hair different ways. This morning it is drawn back tightly into a bun. The taut hair pulls the skin at her temples into smooth ivory planes, and makes her look a little like a lawyer, or perhaps an office manager.

"With whole wheat toast, please."

"Are all of your little students learning to play songs for Christmas?" she asks me.

"They're trying."

"I took lessons when I was a kid but my mother didn't make me practice. I regret it now. I wish I'd practiced."

"Nobody practices."

"Do you ever get Jews?"

"Sometimes."

"Do you make them play Christmas songs?"

"No."

"I don't see your husband much anymore."

"No, not much."

"I mean he's not in here to eat much anymore."

"No."

"I guess he could be in here when I'm not working. You don't have any children, do you?"

"No."

She studies me with bright, curious eyes.

Beside me a Hindu gentleman orders a cheese omelet. He is a professor of civil engineering. The university is just across the street. This is Chicago. I am the blondish woman in the blue coat.

"In America," says the Hindu gentleman, "I like everything except the cold." The skin on his hands is dusky, faintly green.

The waitress can understand how he feels. "Who does!" she says. Then she asks Jascha Heifetz, "Is everything all right?"

Felix Mendelssohn, born Jewish, converted to Christianity and wrote "Hark! The Herald Angels Sing." Actually, it was Mendelssohn's father who converted, probably for business reasons, so that Mendelssohn, a Jew, was born Christian. These things are never easy.

The Hindu gentleman is bringing all of his relatives to America. The waitress, who has seen India's squalor on television, is sympathetic to this venture. "There is some pain in each day," she says. "It's remarkable how life goes on."

"But there is also opportunity." The Hindu gentleman smiles, showing small, perfect teeth. "Americans are too soft."

For reasons I do not completely understand, Junior is not permitted to lay the paper place mat before me, nor to arrange the heavy, whitish silver on the counter. Busboys do not perform these tasks. I toy with the notion that he might one morning exceed his authority, plunge his hands recklessly into the bins of silverware, forks and spoons still moist and warm from the dishwasher. Would this be a catastrophe, or a mishap of lesser magnitude? Does Junior believe his hands are incapable of laying out the silver, that he could as easily take pen and staff paper and compose a sonata? And what would be the consequence of Junior's rash act in the International House of Pancakes? Would the round clock on the wall above the cash register stop in mid-tock and shudder?

22. Which of the following statements about the Classical period of composition are true?

    a. The concept of form achieved great importance.
    b. The works of Haydn and Mozart best exemplify concern for form in music.
    c. The later works of Beethoven predict the breakdown of Classical order.

Chicago's Mayor Jane Byrne understands the breakdown of order. She has moved into the Cabrini-Green housing development. The morning paper shows her arriving at Cabrini-Green in a limousine. "I will stay here," says Mayor Byrne, "until my presence is felt and order is restored. The crime rate in this housing project will go down."

The Hindu gentleman has opened a copy of an Indian newspaper. He taps the crease from the front page with two confident fingers—perhaps the news is good—and turns at once to a back page to read the results of soccer matches.

"Look, Emma," said my old friend and harmony teacher, Professor Wells. "Pick up the Ph.D. and I can get you onto the staff. You ought to be thinking of your future. Private teaching is precarious. Take the GRE and get into a Ph.D. program, and I can get you onto a tenure track."

I wondered who had told him about my husband.

"Emma, what are you now? Thirty?"

"Thirty-three."

"I see."

Junior wears a black apron, made perhaps of vinyl, that

reminds me of pictures I have seen of blacksmiths. He is a member of the True Vine Holiness Church, which he pronounces as one word, true-vine-holiness-church. He tells the waitress, "I had choir practice until ten-thirty last night." The hymn his choir rehearsed was "There Is a Balm in Gilead."

63. Church hymns are often scored beyond the range of average singers. They should be transposed. In what key should the familiar hymn, "There Is a Balm in Gilead," be played to place it in the available range of the average singer?

Beside the bell at my front door is a sign: "Students will please ring once and walk in." But most do not ring at all, they simply walk in.

My husband Tyler made the sign, drawing large black letters on a clean white card, and mounting it in a clear plastic envelope to protect it from the weather. The plastic envelope had originally held a name tag he brought home from a convention. The tag read: "My name is Tyler Nagle," and below that, in red letters, "Yes!"

"Now your students can just ring the bell and walk in," he said. "If you're at the piano with a student and another student comes to the door, you won't have to get up."

"Thank you," I said.

"They can just ring once and walk in."

"Of course."

My students had been walking in right along, but when I married Tyler he began going to the door, greeting each student as if he or she were a guest. Tyler isn't comfortable with children.

First he said, "The hours are odd."

"I can't teach children until school is out."

Then he said, "It's a nuisance, going to the door."

"You don't have to go to the door," I said. "You can sit in the bedroom, and maybe next year we can build onto the house.

It is so small. Perhaps it was a mistake moving into my house instead of your apartment. But where would I have put the piano? Tyler? I love you."

Then he said, "Compelling me to answer the door gives you a feeling of power over me, doesn't it?" Then he made the sign.

84. When two pieces of music in different keys are to be joined (modulation), it is necessary to locate a primary chord held in common by the two keys. Indicate the common chord in the following pairs of keys.

When I was a music student in Memphis I worked as a church organist. This fact amuses Tyler who is a fallen-away Roman Catholic. During this period, someone on the Buildings and Grounds Committee wanted to carpet the church. It was a woman named Pauline Sugrue, or possibly Shurgrue, who wore tailored suits and looked a little like an owl. "Carpeting would be nice," she said, "soft underfoot. Perhaps blue and brown flecked, or a very deep green."

I went to a meeting of the Buildings and Grounds Committee and said, "As soon as you carpet a church, you ruin the organ. The acoustics. It deadens everything, and the sound goes stringy, thready. With so many churches carpeted today, it is almost impossible for people to hear the music as they once did."

The chairman of the committee was a solemn man with tufts of gray hair about his ears. He said, "It's a good thing you came and told us this. Thank you for coming to the meeting tonight."

And Pauline Sugrue, with her owl eyes open very wide said, "We'd have been sorry afterward, when it was too late."

Tyler ate lunch in a church once and charged it to his expense account. He is an excellent salesman, knows how to handle people, tells wonderful stories. "In Baltimore, I finished my call just at noon, so I invited my customer to lunch. He said every Thursday this little Armenian church serves lunch—lamb, pilaf, beer, the works. Afterward, I asked the cashier for a receipt on letterhead. I didn't think they'd have it, but they did. I told her, 'My boss would believe I took a customer to lunch in any bar in town, but an Armenian church?'"

The waitress returns with coffee. "With Jews, what music do they play?"

"They have their own sacred music."

"Even kids? You never hear about it. People never talk about it."

The Hindu gentleman looks up from his paper and considers. "All music began in a religious setting," he says. "Secular music is a modern idea. Every religion has its music."

"Yes, I suppose," says the waitress, "and in a place like this you'd see it all. I mean the university."

The Hindu gentleman raises his eyebrows and then smiles again. "I don't think religion really matters, if you feel good about yourself. Religious music today has mainly historical interest. People now have a variety of emotional outlets, not just religion."

"But I like it," says the waitress, "like Christmas carols. I mean I'm not really religious." She considers this statement, glances at Junior, and lowers her voice. "I mean I don't care a lot one way or the other, but it's interesting, and people never talk about it." She pours coffee into the Hindu gentleman's cup. "You're a real soccer fan, aren't you?"

"Yes," he answers. "I wish it would catch on all over, I mean really catch on." He keeps fit, plays soccer himself on weekends, for the exercise. He believes life in a sluggish, underexercised body is not worth living. "Americans do not take advantage of their opportunities," he says.

"More coffee?" the waitress asks me.

"Just a little, thanks."

"I guess a lot of professional musicians are Jews, aren't they?"

"Yes."

"I guess they'd play any music, professionally I mean. Professionals could play anything they wanted."

"Yes."

"I'd like that," says the waitress. "I wish I could play."

95. Twentieth-century composers have returned to many compositional practices of the earliest (Baroque) composers. All of the following are typical of both twentieth-century and Baroque music. Rank them in importance.

a. Bolder, more realistic in expression.
b. Dissonance (dissonant intervals are admitted).
c. Aleatory, where the player chooses some of the notes to be played.
d. Use of the old church modes (Lydian, Dorian, Phrygian, etc.).

Tyler and I were married in a small church on Halsted Street. Last year, arsonists burned it to the ground. Mayor Jane Byrne has appointed a commission to investigate the alarming increase of arson in Chicago.

"Congratulations, Emma," said Professor Wells. "Welcome aboard. You'll be all right now."

"Yes, thank you."

"You can manage on one income?"

"Yes."

"Of course, you can continue with your private students as well. You enjoy the little ones, don't you?"

"Yes."

"Is the divorce final?"

"Last month."

"And we have a pension plan. I'll be retiring in two years. My wife and I will be moving to Florida."

"I'm sure you look forward to it."

"Emma, you'll be teaching music history. Our classes are quite small. There are so few jobs for musicians today."

The International House of Pancakes has piped-in recorded music, an eclectic array of unobtrusive selections: "Night and Day," "Unforgettable," "Scarborough Fair," "Blue Moon." Somewhere in a recording studio, a sound engineer splices tapes of these songs together, following some principle of programming. Traditionally, the principle for programming music has been to play the oldest first: Baroque, Classical, Romantic, Modern. I don't know which is older, "Night and Day" or "Blue Moon."

Recently, one of my university students said to me, "There is always a scream in Brahms. I understand it technically—it comes from the thickness of the orchestration—but I can't decide if it announces the modern period, or if it is the sound of a wounded thing, dying."

> When you have finished, you may give your examination booklet to the monitor and leave. Please take time to check your work. Although your test scores are not likely to be the predominant factor, the Graduate Record Examinations may nevertheless have an appreciable influence on your important transition to the graduate level of higher education.

When Junior removes dirty dishes from the counter, he leaves the tip in a clean ashtray for the waitress. He is scrupulous about this. Busboys do not receive tips. Junior does not appear to consider this practice abusive. He hums as he busses dishes. The song he hums this morning is "There Is a Balm in Gilead." I button my coat and draw on my gloves. Junior's voice is a bass baritone. To put the melody into his range, he has transposed it into B-flat. When he reaches the end of a verse, he commences the next by gliding smoothly from the tonic B-flat to the fourth at E-flat. The E-flat outlines the dominant seventh harmony, and motivates the return to D. Junior hums with the sure control of a natural musician, bending the time into an expressive *rubato*, then recapturing the beat at the last possible moment.

"You have a very nice voice," I say to him.

"Thank you, miss." Junior grins at me, and I realize for the first time that the piped-in music has stopped. Junior has turned it off. "They don't miss it," he says. "They don't even hear it." I recognize the mischief in his eyes. It is the look that comes over students—the favored few—when they have solved the maze of notes and broken through to the music. Then it is a little like thievery, the leap out of logic, to take a thing or not take it. Frightened a little by the quickened pulse. It is difficult, perhaps as difficult as love. "How many singers are in your choir?"

"Eleven, miss, but I'm the only bass baritone. Not too many people want to sing in choirs anymore."

"No, not too many want to sing, nor to play. Never mind. One strong voice can carry the part."

"Yes, miss."

The waitress pauses, coffee pot in hand, and catches me in her sharp, probing gaze. "Tell your husband hello for me."

"I'll do that."

Beyond the Hindu gentleman, Jascha Heifitz has not moved. Perhaps he is thinking of all the music he has recorded, a small mountain of records: Schubert's "Ave Maria"; the Hebrew "Kol Nidrei" set by the Lutheran Bruch; Bach's "Kom Susser Tod." Perhaps he is recalling the ovation he received when he played Mendelssohn's Violin Concerto in New York for the first time, a little Jewish boy fresh from St. Petersburg. I pause for a moment beside him. At close range, his pale skin is gray, the color of stone.

Across the room, Junior looks up from his work and smiles. "Have a nice day!" he calls to me.

"Thank you," I call back from the doorway. "Thank you very much."

All Kinds of Flowers

"My father was a scholar," says Diana Jean, "and a scientist."

"He was two things?" I ask. In English you can change a statement into a question by simply raising your voice. People who are not native speakers sometimes say this makes the language unstable. I say you have to work at it.

"He was a physicist," she says. Diana Jean, despite her name, is German. She has large gray eyes that stare and seem never to blink. The staring eyes make her look cold, almost calculating, but I believe she is only near-sighted, and has chosen not to wear glasses out of vanity. She is sitting at my kitchen table drawing a tea bag back and forth through a mug of hot water. Her decision to forego glasses was not a wise one. The hard naked eyes make her look older, not younger. Is she thirty? I am older, perhaps old enough to be her mother.

"When he died," says Diana Jean, "my brother was going to throw away his Ph.D. thesis." Her throw emerges as trow, her thesis as tee-sus, but she believes her English is improving.

"Your father's thesis or your brother's?" I ask. I try to recall the subject of this conversation, and I cannot. I do not think it was fathers.

Diana Jean has been staring at her tea. Now she looks up, perplexed. She looks first at her husband, then at me, then at my husband.

"Was your brother going to throw away your father's thesis

or his own?" I smile to show her I have her best interest at heart.

"My father's thesis. My brother has no thesis. He is only a teacher." Diana Jean also smiles. I am the wife of her husband's boss, and she is required to please me.

Diana Jean's mother named her for a character in a novel. That is why she does not have a regular German name like Gretchen or possibly Thekla. She has told me which novel it was but I no longer remember the title, nor do I remember why Diana Jean and her husband have stopped by our house this Saturday afternoon.

Diana Jean now rotates the tea bag slowly in the hot water. "But I did not let him," she says. The liquid grows darker, brown and then black. The movement of her hand seems relentless. She is brewing a very ugly cup of tea. I study her face for a sign. Is she repelled by the mug of bitter tea before her? She gives no sign.

"What?" I ask.

Diana Jean smiles again. "I did not let my brother throw away my father's thesis." She is glad I am helping her with her English.

Many Europeans like weak tea. They like loose tea brewed in a pot. When they are served a tea bag, they must have a saucer. Then they can lift the bag out as soon as the water turns a pale amber, and place the bag on the saucer. I have not served Diana Jean a saucer, and I watch to see how she will cope with this small crisis.

I do not completely understand the complexities of our relationship, how I came to be the superior of this small blonde woman who is sitting at my table. I lean forward, rest an elbow on the table, run my right hand over my left forearm, examining the flesh for signs of superiority, and find none. I wonder what would happen if I suddenly said, I'm in charge here. Would everyone laugh? Would Diana Jean laugh?

I am drinking coffee. My husband and the husband of

Diana Jean are also drinking coffee. Americans are coffee drinkers, but most Americans keep a few tea bags on hand. Americans are hospitable. This is common knowledge.

Diana Jean understands our relationship perfectly. If I asked her to explain it to me, I believe she would open her black leather purse, take out a notebook, and draw a small map for me. It would be in perfect scale. Diana Jean would write across the top of it, this map is in perfect scale.

This is how I know I am the superior of Diana Jean. She lifts the dripping tea bag from the mug and places it on a paper napkin. On the white napkin, the wet bag sends out brown creeping stains. Diana Jean looks at the stains sadly, and takes responsibility for them. I am held blameless. That is how I know.

"What was it on?" asks my husband. He is a tall man who wears wire-rimmed glasses. He is never petty. We have been married a long time.

"What?" asks Diana Jean. Each time my husband asks her a question, Diana Jean says, what? She wishes to understand completely any questions asked by her husband's boss before attempting to answer them.

"What subject did your father write his thesis on?" asks my husband. He is a businessman. He likes to get the facts, but he is never petty.

"I don't know," says Diana Jean. "It was about physics. He was a physicist."

"Diana Jean has about fourteen kinds of tea at home," says her husband whose name is Fred. He is a plump, boyish-looking man who is always prepared to laugh. "She goes through all of them, tea, tea, tea." Fred laughs heartily. I try to think of fourteen kinds of tea, and I cannot. Black, green, iced, spiced. Tea in a blue cup. Tea in Chicago, in New York, in Amsterdam.

Recently my husband inserted the following anecdote in the monthly newsletter he distributes to the employees of his business:

On KLM Royal Dutch Airlines, flight attendants seem to begin all of their English sentences with this phrase: "Passengers will have the possibility to . . . ." Eat, drink, sleep, purchase. "Passengers will have the possibility to view these recent magazines. They will have the possibility to read them in either Dutch or English."

Americans find this amusing for a time. Then they tire of it. they are likely to say, "Oh miss, there is a much simpler way to say that."

Let them try it! The attendant will smile—one of those formidable, robust Dutch smiles—and reply, "But that is how *we* speak English!"

Damn stubborn Dutch, says my husband. Lord, I should know. If anybody should know, it's me.

Although I was born in Utrecht, I have no accent. I have lived in America so long I speak idiomatic, unaccented English. I can say, those yahoos are in cahoots. I can say, the tables are turned. I can say, these three seen through the tree are thirsty. But I still dream in Holland Dutch. *Een landschap van dichtbij*. Diana Jean, with her accent, thinks I am a rich American.

Fred helps himself to more coffee from the big aluminum pot. Fred was born in Detroit. He is a friendly fellow.

"My father bought me my car before he died," Diana Jean says, "so I always take care of it because . . . well, I did not wash it today, but I usually do, and vacuum it. You can understand what I mean?" She smiles. We all understand.

Fred understands. He leans forward over his coffee understandingly and explains: He did not know someone was going to give his wife a new car. He wonders how many other people's wives were ever given new cars. Probably so. It probably happens a lot. There is nothing wrong with it. What the heck?

Diana Jean's car is bright green. She tells Fred when he may drive it, and takes it to a special mechanic for tune-ups. Fred's own car is a rusty black sedan, but he does not mind. Not at all. Many people have cars that look much like his.

"Is it a four cylinder or a six?" asks my husband. He will make all of the proper determinations, just as soon as he has the facts. When he knows how many cylinders Diana Jean's car has, he may be able to tell her the subject of her father's thesis.

"What?" asks Diana Jean.

"Six," says Fred.

"Six cylinders," says Diana Jean.

I am embarrassed for my husband. Did he really believe a German physicist about to die would give his daughter a green car with only four cylinders?

Fred met and married Diana Jean while he was stationed in Germany with the American army. The story of Fred's army service and his courtship is hilariously funny, but complex. To understand it, you must know about American army ranks, like specialist first class. This is the third or fourth time I have heard the story and I still do not know when to laugh. Briefly, although it is not a brief story, Fred was being paid very generous wages because he held a high rank, but he was only doing a menial job for these wages. In this manner, Fred outfoxed the whole American army, the whole damned army. They paid him all that money and never knew what hit them. Fred suspects that never again in his lifetime will he achieve such—what word should he use—greatness?

While Fred was robbing the army, he met and married Diana Jean. Before the marriage, Fred promised her father he would earn a degree in physics. Back in the U.S., he told the old man, with the G.I. benefits. No sweat. It was a sincere promise.

The wedding took place in the garden of his bride's home. It was summer and flowers were blooming. There was a table laden with rich German food. If you looked up from the table you could see a blue mountain with its peak lost in the clouds. Fred remembers the mountain. He remembers the food. For Fred, robbing the army and getting married blend into one memory. It has—what should he say—rightness?

But Fred did not earn a degree in physics. It was not his style, really. The old guy understood that. Instead, Fred went to night school for three semesters.

"Three semesters," says Diana Jean, and glances sharply at my husband. Each time Fred tells the story and says three semesters, Diana Jean also says three semesters.

"More tea?" my husband asks Diana Jean. He smiles to reassure her. The boss knows about the three semesters. Fred's educated. The boss won't forget. My husband gives her more hot water and a saucer for her tea bag.

Fred is here to drop off a report. There is a brown envelope on the table between Fred and my husband. The report is in the envelope. I remember the report quite clearly now.

"Thank you," says Diana Jean. "I like tea. I enjoy it." She thanks my husband by fluttering one hand. The hand is ornamented with two valuable rings. One is set with a large diamond. The second is an emerald set with small diamonds. The rings belonged to her mother. The mother is dead. Diana Jean is also wearing an attractive, old-fashioned gold wristwatch. It too belonged to her mother.

"Did you get your jewelry photographed?" I ask Diana Jean. I have now remembered what I should say to this woman, the appropriate subject. Many people in authority, like me, keep card files to help them remember things. They keep one card for each person they know. I have never kept a card file, but I could. I know how card files work. A typical card might say: Smith, John, allergic to oysters, studied at Pepperdine, puts sugar in his coffee, collects stamps but has all of the common ones.

When people in authority appear tactful, it may simply mean they have consulted their card files.

"I am having trouble operating the camera," says Diana Jean. It was her father's camera. It is very valuable, and also complicated to operate. Her father took prizewinning photographs of flowers. The flowers may have been azaleas or shasta daisies. Diana Jean has told us which flowers they were but I have forgotten. If she tells us again I will write down the names of the flowers. I could write them on a white card or even on one of the paper napkins. Azalea. Shasta daisy. I wonder if I should say, Diana Jean, do you mind if I write down the names of the flowers? Or just slip a napkin out of the stack and do it? Which is the proper procedure for a person in authority? The napkins belong to me.

Diana Jean says, "My father told me to photograph all of the jewelry for the insurance, in case anything is stolen. My mother died before my father."

My father died before my mother. I could say this, but I do not.

Fred leans forward eagerly to take us into his confidence. "There's several thousand dollars worth of jewelry." He would not tell this to just anyone, but the boss and his wife are special. He does not remember he has already told us about the valuable jewelry. Fred is proud of Diana Jean, glances at us from time to time to see if we're taking it all in. What the heck? There's nothing wrong with it.

"That worked out pretty well," says my husband. "Your father gave you the camera to photograph your mother's jewelry."

"My father died before he could teach me to operate the camera," says Diana Jean. "It has caused me a lot of trouble."

I cannot imagine anyone robbing Diana Jean of her jewelry. I try to picture dark, burly figures drawing around her, tearing the rings from her hand, the watch from her slender wrist. I picture her sleeping in her bed in a filmy green nightdress, the same shade of green as her car, while thieves slip into her bedroom and rifle her jewelry box. This effort is not successful. The pictures are static. The thieves do not look like thieves. They look like the members of Fred's bowling team, the team he is now telling us about. Fred believes his team will win a championship and travel to a distant city to compete in a bowl-off.

Diana Jean says, "I am glad Fred is on the bowling team. Exercise keeps him fit."

Fred smiles. To think that bowling, which he loves, can also be good for him. Somehow, Diana Jean is responsible for all his good fortune.

"Do you want to take that tea bag out of the water," my husband asks, "and put it on that saucer?" My husband was born in Illinois. His parents still live there in a white house. His mother's jewelry is not valuable and is not insured. "Maybe I should start bowling again," says my husband, glancing at the brown envelope. He is glad Fred has brought the report. "I used to bowl."

Diana Jean smiles encouragement at the boss. "Exercise is just as important as diet for keeping fit." Then she quickly adds, "Of course, you are very fit already."

"I used to bowl around one-forty," my husband says.

"Yeah," says Fred, "you should."

Diana Jean says that she herself does not bowl. I wonder if it is because the fingers with the rings would not fit into the holes of the bowling ball. She would have to take off the rings, and where could she lay them that a thief would not find them? She could scarcely say to a passerby, excuse me, you have a honest face, will you hold these valuable rings while I bowl? She could lock them into the glove compartment of the green car, but cars are stolen all the time. Perhaps Fred would hold them for her. Here, I'll hold your rings for you while you bowl, honey. But I do not think she would trust the rings to Fred. If only her father had not died before he could teach her to operate his camera. If only Fred had earned a degree in physics.

Fred says the city where the bowl-off will be held is St.

Louis. "The team will go by train," he says. He is looking forward to the train ride. "I've only ridden on trains a time or two," he says. "Once or twice."

I have ridden on trains many times. I have ridden on many trains. I could say this, but I don't.

On Dutch trains, even today, conductors rarely ask passengers to show their tickets. This happens everywhere in Holland. Amsterdam, Rotterdam, Utrecht, Haarlem, The Hague. People visiting Holland from other countries are puzzled by this practice. They say, passengers should show their tickets. Dishonest people may be riding free. They fear Dutch society may collapse at any moment. They make helpful suggestions. They return home and tell their friends which things in Holland need improvement. But they always add that Holland is the only country in Europe where you can get a free glass of water to drink in a restaurant. I am not sure this is completely true, but the water in Dutch restaurants has become very famous, perhaps as famous as the water of the Zuider Zee. This is the new Holland. Today there is a Burger King opposite the railroad station in Amsterdam. It features the Whopper.

I have never asked a German waiter for a glass of water. Perhaps he would bring it with a cheerful smile. Perhaps he would serve it to me with a graceful flourish. He might say, it's free, no charge, speaking in fine, idiomatic, unaccented English.

Diana Jean removes her tea bag from her mug of water and arranges it in the exact center of the saucer. This creates a small model of the solar system. The tea bag is the sun. Everything revolves about the sun. There is a thin gold line around the edge of the saucer. Everything revolves so fast. Everything in the world has blurred into a thin gold line. The tea bag and the saucer are an illustration from a physics textbook.

I have seen the old movies about the war on television. They are misleading. In them, the German soldiers are brutal, and very rude. During the occupation of Holland, when I was a small child, the German soldiers were usually courteous to civilians. They were disciplined. On Sunday mornings, a military band stood in the square of the Dom Kerk in Utrecht and played religious music. Dutch people said, see how straight they stand! And they never talk back to the bandmaster! In every German home, there is always a whip hanging on the back of the door.

My husband says, you know that isn't true, not really. You never saw the inside of a German home. Please, you're only hurting yourself. Try.

Dutch people said, there is not a whip in all of Holland. Not one.

When the Dutch knew the Germans were really coming, everyone said, we will open the dikes! We will wash the dirty Germans with Dutch water! But the plan failed. The dikes were not opened.

What the old movies fail to show is that the real menace of war, for most people, is hunger. During the occupation, we lived by barter, my mother and father, my brother and I. Before the war our home held many lovely objects, candlesticks, brass bookends, china plates, a silver coffee pot. My mother had a gold wedding ring and a diamond engagement ring. She had a gold watch. It hung from her neck on a gold chain.

Diana Jean was not born until after the war, but she knows

all about it. She has told us about the war. She learned about it in the modern German schools. The war was very sad, says Diana Jean sadly.

The first winter of the occupation brought little real hardship to the Dutch because the Germans were winning the war. With the onset of the second winter, everything changed. The German army began to lose. Shortages developed. The army took the food from the occupied countries. They sent it back to Germany, to feed the German people.

My husband says, look, you don't actually know that. Let go of it, for your own sake.

I say, I saw Dutch potatoes going on a German ship. Were you there?

Although my father did not photograph flowers, he was a tender-hearted man. He said to my mother, you choose. Then my mother would select a candlestick or a china plate. Later it was a pair of shoes or a winter coat. Then my father would ride his bicycle into the country to barter for food with Dutch farmers. During the second winter, my father died of pneumonia. There was no longer any medicine in Holland, no coal, no soap.

In Holland, when butchers dress rabbits, it is their custom to leave one of each animal's feet intact. This is a courtesy to customers, to assure them they are not buying cats. During the war, some people ate cats.

My husband says, look, I knew a butcher in Illinois who tried the same thing. People are the same all over. How can you trust your memory when you were so young? I love you, isn't that enough? What does it accomplish?

After my father died, it was my brother's job to search for food. He was fourteen. He would pack objects into his rucksack and ride my father's bicycle into the country searching for farmers who might still have hidden potatoes, who might still want a worn pair of shoes. One day he was stopped on the road and beaten, and the bicycle was stolen. After that, he walked into the country. The people who beat my brother were Dutch. They were not German. Many people were on the roads then, walking or on bicycles. One day my brother brought back an egg. He had packed it into his sack with dry leaves to keep it from breaking. The egg did not break.

"Diana Jean," I ask, "what kind of flowers did your father photograph?" I had thought my husband would ask this question, but he has not, and I can't wait forever.

"All kinds," says Diana Jean. "He photographed all kinds of flowers."

"I believe you told me they were azaleas."

"Azaleas?" asks Diana Jean.

"And shasta daisies."

She pauses with her mug of tea halfway to her lips. She blinks once.

"Here we are at last!" I say. "'By lost ways, by a nod, by words.'" Archibald MacLeish was the first poet I read in English. He said, let's call a spade a spade. He meant Ezra Pound and fascism. Later, I also read Pound. These things aren't easy, but I'm in no hurry. "Diana Jean," I say, "I'm in no hurry about any of this. Do you want to try to remember the names of the flowers?"

She stares silently at the tea bag resting on the saucer. Perhaps she is translating English into German and back again. Linguists say that English, structurally, is closer to Holland Dutch than to any other language. Structure ignores the difficulties of pronunciation, the Dutch gutturals and the

English apicals, but there could be something to it. Perhaps I have some small advantage.

Then the mug of tea comes to rest gently on the table, and Diana Jean smiles again. "My father photographed all kinds of flowers."

It is my husband who takes things in hand. "What kind of film did he use?" he asks.

When my brother was beaten, five of his teeth were knocked out. My mother wept over the lost teeth, almost silently. "He is an old man at fourteen," she said softly. "Permanent teeth will not grow back." That was the day my mother lost hope, not later when there was nothing left in our house to barter, when my brother began stealing food.

"What?" asks Diana Jean.

"She doesn't know," says Fred.

"I wish he had told me what kind of film he used," says Diana Jean. "I wish he had told me before he died."

"I'm going to buy a new bowling ball," says Fred. He's certain his team will win. "When I get to St. Louis, I'm going to go up in the Arch. You ride up in an elevator that follows the curve of it. When you're up in the top, you can look right down into the baseball park, but you don't see much unless there's a home game that day."

The city of Utrecht was liberated by Canadian soldiers. My brother, breathless, brought us the news. "The Canadians love little children! I will take Anna to beg from them! The soldiers have food!"

"Please," my mother said, "she is so small."

Then my brother took my mother gently by the shoulders. "Mama," he said, "there is not a scrap of food left in Holland. The Red Cross is coming but they cannot get through Belgium. It could be days, weeks. Mama, look at us! We will be dead by then! The soldiers will not give food to me, not to a man!"

"Then I will come too," said my mother.

They took me to a place where Canadian soldiers were camped. My mother and my brother hid in a hedgerow. "Anna," my brother said to me, "walk among the soldiers. Call out can-dee! Call out very loud."

"I cannot," I whispered. My throat was locked shut with fear.

"But you can!" said my brother. "My brave sister can!"

I walked among the soldiers. I called out can-dee. The soldiers gave me candy. They gave me tins of food. They did this for the sake of all the little girls back home in Canada.

"The Arch," says Diana Jean, "symbolizes the gateway to the West." She has studied American history, believes Americans should be good citizens. "Pioneers gathered there and made up wagon trains."

"I'll definitely go up in the Arch," says Fred.

Diana Jean says it is time for them to go. "Thank you for the tea," she says. "Thank you for the coffee."

"This sure was nice," says Fred, "but it's late."

I did not know it was late, and now I wonder what time it is. I could ask Diana Jean. I could say, Diana Jean, what time is it? *Wie spät ist es?* This would compel her to raise her wrist, raise it close to the cold, near-sighted eyes, and read her mother's wristwatch. I could do this. I'm in charge. But I don't. "You're welcome, Diana Jean," I say. You're welcome is an English idiom. It puzzles foreigners because the words have no real content.

But Diana Jean is onto it. She smiles. Her English is improving all the time. Soon she will learn to say, there's room at the top. She will learn to say thirteen, and yellow Jello.

"I'm glad you came by," says my husband. He smiles at me.

40

"My wife is glad you came by." We have been married a long time.

"What time is it?" I ask my husband.

"Four-thirty," he says, consulting his wristwatch, "four-thirty on the dot."

Energy

O n the day he learned his son was planning to quit high
school, Grafmiller ran out of gas on the expressway.
Rolf, seventeen and his only child, lived with Grafmiller's former wife. For a moment her phone call had surprised him,
then it seemed the next inevitable step in a pattern of decline.

Nothing was going well for Grafmiller. His office had installed a computer that worked erratically; when the main
trunk from the home office in St. Louis broke down, his work
had to wait, sometimes for hours. His car had serious trans-
mission trouble. He no longer knew what his dreams meant.
He'd become interested in his dreams in college while reading Carl Jung's autobiography, and had kept a journal of them
from time to time since. He took keen satisfaction in watching
his own inner narrative unfold and fancied he was good at
spotting tendencies in himself, keeping his life on an even
keel. Now everything seemed gibberish. He had dreamed, for
example, that workmen were enclosing the shopping mall
near his home. In the center of the mall was a building that
resembled a small Greek temple, but also looked a bit like an
animal cage. He had never seen such a building in real life. In
the dream, the foreman was explaining to him that this building would not be torn down as originally planned. Rather, a
new structure would be bolted onto its roof. The bolts the
workmen were using resembled the headbolts on his automobile engine. Grafmiller suspected the dream had something to do with his most primitive instincts, and that one

way or another he was being buried, but it really made no sense to him.

He had been seeing a woman from his office, Rochelle, and found he no longer took pleasure in the association. At thirty-eight she was not really young, but still four years younger than Grafmiller himself, and pretty enough, with a short rather buxom figure, neat brown hair that was surprisingly soft to his touch, and large quite beautiful hands. He had found her sensitive and intelligent. Only a short time ago their liaison had seemed perfectly pleasant and he'd thought of asking her to marry him, but now their walks and little suppers had become desultory, their couplings mechanical, even stifling. Once, lying in her arms, his face nuzzled against her neck, Grafmiller had felt he could not get his breath, and had pulled away suddenly, leaving Rochelle, nude and disheveled, lying across the bed looking ridiculous, like an old woman who had slipped and fallen.

Into this malaise had come the phone call from his former wife (one more thing, always one more thing).

"You'll have to talk to Rolf."

"Of course. Give me a few days to organize my thoughts."

"You can't put it off." Her tone laid blame squarely on the father.

He accepted it without argument. "Of course."

In fact, what he had sought to organize these four days were thoughts about himself, the order and magnitude of his failures. He saw a pattern: beginning, growing, culminating in the trouble with his son. (*Failing*, an archaic term from childhood. When the elderly—Grafmiller pictured a man—began their measured march toward death, drying, shrinking, slipping into confusion, people of his parents' generation had said, "He is failing.")

Now, driving through the bleak March night toward the apartment Rolf shared with his mother, Grafmiller found himself doubting all of his certainties, inverting everything and giving it its opposite meaning. Although he had been divorced for years and had never managed to establish a really close relationship with Rolf, he felt a strong commitment to the boy. He had invested much of his own emotion in his hopes for his son. Hadn't he tried to do his best, event by event, across the years? Then it seemed to him that this was precisely what was wrong, that his association with his son had been a series of disconnected incidents that added up to nothing. As he pulled into the driveway he wondered (of all things) if he truly loved the boy, and he thought for one giddy moment that everything in his head was going to spin like a slot machine, then stop suddenly and reveal some terrible truth. This thought was somehow connected to his drawing suddenly away from Rochelle and again, sitting in his car, he experienced a brief sensation of suffocation.

"Come in," said his former wife. Pale, blondish, she had been thin and angular for many years. He could not now recall ever having felt passion for her. He felt no animosity toward her either. She worked in an office, as he did, and it seemed to Grafmiller they now had more in common than when they had been married. They both rose in the morning and went to work, budgeted their money, shopped on the way home, felt alarm over the cost of things, were concerned for Rolf. She was a little like a sister to him. Neither had remarried. Now, silhouetted in the doorway, she looked old to Grafmiller, older than Rochelle, and weary from her day's work.

Rolf appeared behind her. He was already an inch taller than his father but thin, like his mother, and more delicately constructed. To Grafmiller's surprise, the boy seemed animated. He came forward with an eager smile, both hands outstretched. "Dad! Can we go out? I want to take you someplace."

"Certainly," said Grafmiller, welcoming this joy although he had no idea what it involved.

His former wife sighed lightly and smiled a little. She continued to look tired.

Rolf found a denim jacket with the sleeves torn out. Graf-miller supposed it matched his faded jeans. He put the jacket on over a T-shirt that was decorated with splashes of iridescent paint. His limp hair, dark like Grafmiller's own, hung nearly to his shoulders, and he wore a headband of sorts that made him look a little like a farmer. Grafmiller thought the boy needed a warmer coat for the chilly night, but said nothing, not wishing to begin the evening on a critical note.

Rolf directed him to drive to a nightclub in a seedy section of the city. "It's pretty early but we can stay awhile. We've got all evening, right, Dad?"

"Right," Grafmiller said guardedly. He had expected they would be having a talk about the value of completing Rolf's education, but the boy's joy was contagious. Grafmiller felt good for the first time in days. He decided there would be time enough later to talk.

The club was in an old automobile showroom. The large front windows had been painted green. They were meant to suggest a forest of palm trees. The bar near the entrance was nearly deserted at this early hour. The few patrons and the bartender greeted Rolf with friendly nods. Rolf led Grafmiller to a small, round table near the empty bandstand—all of the other tables were empty—and a waitress in a leather skirt and vest immediately brought them two glasses of wine. "This is my father!" Rolf said to her.

"Wow!" said the young woman. "Oh wow, your father!" She grinned and rolled her eyes upward as if Grafmiller's presence was too much to be believed. Grafmiller looked at the wine—Rolf was not legally old enough to be served—and decided to say nothing.

"Dad, I've got all these things to ask you." Rolf leaned forward, tense now and excited. "There were musicians in your family, right? And artists? A dancer? I asked Mom, over and over; there's no one in her family. Nothing. Nobody."

Grafmiller's reaction to this, even before he took time to

46

sort it out, was that his former wife had been having a hard time of it; Rolf had his mother under some sort of concerted siege. This sort of thing probably happened often. The mother was the boy's most convenient target. He, Grafmiller, had probably not been sufficiently sympathetic to her position. "Hmm," he said now to his son, "artists, musicians." He wondered if mother and son were both coming at him, but from slightly different angles, *triangulation*. The word made him think of strangulation and he wondered for a moment if he might have another attack of breathlessness.

"You know, Dad, you told me about an uncle who played the guitar and had these special talents." Rolf's manner was urgent; he was growing irritated.

"Oh yes, my Uncle David. His special talents were with bees. He raised bees and could take honey off without being stung."

"No!" Rolf cried. "On the guitar! You told me that!"

People were drifting in now. Grafmiller noted they were all young, many as young as Rolf. No one seemed to be over twenty-five. Musicians were setting up equipment on the jerry-built stage.

"He wrote songs!" Rolf persisted. "Don't you remember that?"

"Yes, he did." Grafmiller was going on instinct, reluctant to lose the earlier camaraderie with his son. He vaguely remembered that his Uncle David had made up songs, played a guitar. He had probably told Rolf that.

"I mean," said Rolf, "it probably didn't seem like much to you before. That's why you forgot."

"I'm sure that's it," said Grafmiller, grateful for the boy's conciliatory tone.

"And somebody danced. You said when you played in the attic as a child there was a ballerina costume, and shoes."

"That was my sister," Grafmiller said cautiously. His sister had taken dancing lessons, perhaps for a year.

One of the musicians, carrying a guitar, approached the table. From a distance and in the dim light of the club he

47

looked dissipated, in outlandish clothes and with his face heavily rouged. Closer, Grafmiller saw he was actually a boy only a little older than Rolf. His costume was vaguely Middle Eastern, loose wine-colored bloomers, a lime green shirt, bands of metal on his arms.

"Hey!" Rolf cried out. "Meet my dad!"

A smile broke from behind the makeup. "God, your dad!" Grafmiller shook hands with the boy. "God, that's really great! I can't imagine bringing my dad here. But you're from a musical family, Mr. Grafmiller. Rolf told us all about you. That would figure."

The room was filling with customers. Other young people approached and Grafmiller realized he had become the center of attention. He felt like an overweight, middle-aged Buddha being adored. Rolf beamed.

"Look, Mr. Grafmiller," said the guitarist, "you gotta hear this now. After all, that's what you came for."

"Yeah, yeah," said someone in the group.

"We'll do 'Eyes' first," said the guitarist. "That's the blockbuster."

Rolf reddened. "Whatever you guys think."

The guitarist and three other musicians in similar gaudy attire assembled on the bandstand. They were two guitarists, a drummer, and a young man in a leather tunic who now appeared to be the vocalist. A blast of sound, painfully loud, erupted and Grafmiller strained to understand the words. Rolf quickly drew a songsheet from his pocket and thrust it at his father. Grafmiller read at the top, "'Eyes,' Words and Music by Rolf Grafmiller," and then could decipher that the vocalist was shouting:

> Eyes . . . eyes
> The eyes of crowds
> Look back at me
> From midnight mirrors.
> In each falling tear I see

48

Reflections of ecstasy
Lost in tears
Forever lost in tears.

Then it was all repeated with slight variations, in a monotone and at intense volume. Young people squirmed all about
them, dancing and moaning as if in religious fervor. Grafmiller felt cast adrift and pretended careful concentration on
the printed lyric to give himself time to get his bearings.
"Eyes" was followed by "Alone," to which it bore a marked
resemblance. Rolf's images of melancholy and alienation
pounded against Grafmiller's ears, assaulted his mind. The
variations on "Alone" continued for a very long time.

When the musicians ended the set, they gathered once
again around Grafmiller's table. He knew they were waiting
for him to speak and chose his words carefully. "The songs
have . . . tremendous energy," he said, "real vigor. I don't
think I've ever heard anything quite like them." He wondered
if Rolf would detect his guarded tone.

But the boy was too excited to notice. "I knew you'd like
them, Dad! I knew it!"

"Yeah," said the first guitarist, "Rolf said that. He really did!"

Grafmiller felt his breath catch, his throat close momen-
tarily, and held the table firmly to avoid panic. "I have to
admit I don't understand the music very well."

"Jesus!" said the young vocalist. "That's nothing! We hardly
understand it ourselves. Rolf's way ahead of his time. This
son of yours is so damned creative! When the rest of us look
ahead, we just see shadows, but Rolf sees it all. He turns this
stuff out so fast, over and over!"

Rolf was embarrassed. He tried to look earnest. "But you get
it, Dad. With your instincts, I knew you'd *get* the music."

Grafmiller nodded slowly. He wondered if they were going
to ask him for money.

"You know, Dad," Rolf continued, "it's about the individual
in society, about all the pain."

"That's it," said the drummer. "That's all there is today, pain. That's what Rolf sees so clearly."

"The music has energy," Grafmiller said again, and wished he had not, but they really did not seem to be listening to him. "What are your plans?" he asked Rolf. "You don't even play an instrument."

"I'm learning guitar."

"Is he ever!" the guitarist offered. "You never saw anybody learn so fast in your life! Another month, we'll put him up on stage. That's where he belongs."

A sudden perversity swept over Grafmiller. "I suppose you need money," he said. He had none to give them, and the sooner they knew it the better.

But they shook their heads. "We've got club dates, Dad," said Rolf, "some really good bookings. They're getting better all the time. That'll finance demo tapes."

The guitarist nodded vigorously. "And if we don't have an album out in six months. . . ." He shrugged, too overcome to finish the sentence.

Grafmiller began to chuckle, and then to laugh uncontrollably, until his shoulders shook and tears appeared in his eyes. Rolf had brought him to this place seeking his approval, nothing more. The thought was incredibly clean, pure, beautiful, ridiculous, hilarious. He began to tremble and could not stop.

"It's emotion," said the young waitress who had started patting his back as if he were choking. "Jesus, that music does the same thing to me, every time."

"My father is a very sensitive person," Rolf said gravely.

Someone gave him a tissue and Grafmiller wiped his eyes, blew his nose. He wondered why his former wife had given him no warning. Had she said to Rolf, "We will just let your father see this spectacle for himself"? He felt certain she had. He could imagine it, see her standing with her hands on her scrawny hips, suffering with her pained, martyr's face, a face he now brought back to mind perfectly across the years.

He could not be certain if the powerful, exhilarating feelings rising in him came out of spite for her or from participation in his son's joy. It occurred to him they might even have been roused by the music. He took in breath slowly, fully, and felt it course through his lungs, felt the beating of his heart. "I'm speechless," he said, and sat back in his chair.

The young people were satisfied. They turned their faces on him as one person and smiled . . . at Rolf's latest success, his father. Grafmiller smiled too.

Bargaining

The student symphony orchestra of Hollingsworth College is rehearsing Johann Strauss's "Tales from the Vienna Woods." Passing through the broad front hall of the music building, on her way to the small cubicle that serves her as office and studio, Amelia hears the hollow fifths of the introduction through the closed double doors of the orchestra room. The French horns agonize over the initial eighth notes that are meant to sparkle like silver fish leaping into morning's first light. Following this, the clarinets grope in panic for the dotted half note. Amelia knows most of these students. All music majors at Hollingsworth must have keyboard skills, and Amelia teaches piano. The Strauss transcription the players have been given, a Romantic extravaganza, is too difficult for them. This has been going on for two weeks.

Amelia is unable to pass by without looking through the thick window at this scene of torment and humiliation. The violins have lost all of their vibrato. They go at the broken thirds of the first theme with weary, sagging bows. The boy at the percussionist's post droops on his stool. Only the first cellist, a pale girl with auburn hair, has mastered her part. Her sharp, brilliant attack is a reprimand to the sufferers around her. She presses her lips into a tight pucker of concern as she plays. This expression seems meant to assure the others she is still their friend, to tell them she wishes mightily the world had been made in some different way.

Amelia is young but she is already more teacher than

performer. She does not recall making a conscious decision about this, thinks she probably grew into teaching and away from performing by a series of small steps, many small decisions.

The conductor of the student orchestra this year is a new assistant professor, a middle-aged man named James Stapher, or perhaps Stapole. Amelia met him only once, at a faculty gathering in the fall. An intense, joyless man with round black eyes, he is an abominable teacher. He stands stiffly before his music stand, always in a gray suit, conducting with his hands, making pencil notations on his score from time to time. When he talks to the players, his pencil draws figures in the air as if he were writing words on a large public sign.

In some way Amelia does not completely understand, the conductor turns this musical disaster to his advantage. His fluent hands proclaim that he is made of better stuff than these students, has come from a finer place, tolerates their blundering only through some largesse of spirit. The persistent whine of his voice promises to lead the players out of their shameful ineptitude.

But the students have lost all faith in his promises. They sit stupidly as he talks, hot and miserable, the noon sun flooding over them from a wall of windows, glum prisoners who have lost all autonomy and abandoned every hope.

Amelia watches, then draws back firmly from the temptation to plunge into sentimentality. These students carry no stones of irrevocable tragedy at their hearts. They will be set blessedly free in another twenty minutes. They will make sport of this man behind his back. She stands one moment more, cultivating this fine sense of detachment. She brushes imaginary hair from her forehead and marvels at the way her hand rises in one perfect arc to perform this task.

At the turn in the hallway Mrs. Mills, the cheerful white-headed woman who types for the music faculty, greets

Amelia pleasantly. "How well you look today, Mrs. Perlingiero! The color's come back into your cheeks."

"Yes, I'm fine," says Amelia. "Quite."

"Your first student is early again," Mrs. Mills says softly. "Such a dedicated young man. He wanted to be let in to practice so I unlocked your door. I knew you wouldn't mind."

"Of course. Thank you, Mrs. Mills."

Amelia finds the sight of the white placard held to her door by a thin brass frame unsettling: Amelia Morehouse Perlingiero. Assistant Professor. Piano. She wonders why her name seems a shameful, arrogant thing. At the edge of her mind she is engaged in an intense conversation, as if bargaining with someone. With Mrs. Mills, perhaps? With James Stapole? With the red-haired cellist? There are fragments of words she cannot quite grasp. This hum of sound seems always to be present. Has it been so for only two months? She cannot now recall a time when it was not there. When she was a little girl practicing Hanon on the old upright piano in the living room, it had not occurred to her she might grow up to be a professor of music who was not entirely sane. Did voices hum at the edge of her mind even then? *But I have only been ill!* she protests silently. *I am recovering!* The wraiths in her head brush aside this declaration, the bargaining continues unabated. To steady herself, Amelia focuses on a memory, the monotonous ripple of Hanon on the ancient, never-tuned family piano, and opens the door.

Daniel leaps up from the bench like a tightly coiled spring suddenly released, breaking off midway in a Chopin waltz. "Professor Perlingiero! I know I'm a nuisance like this!" Daniel is fretful, intense, frail as a shadow.

"It's all right, Daniel. It's fine. I'm glad to see you."

"I listened to Ashkenazy's recording all week," says Daniel, "and now I wish I hadn't. It was the wrong thing to do. Now I'm just parroting the sounds and not hearing the music at all. I knew it would happen! Everyone says it will. You told

me, 'Listen to the record but don't memorize the interpreta-
tion '" He hands back the record he has borrowed from her
and seats himself at the piano. These existential dilemmas
consume Daniel. He confronts hard choices courageously
and discovers each time, belatedly, that all of his reasoning
has been based on bad faith.

"Let's try another waltz, Daniel. Let's have a breath of fresh
air." This is a poor choice of words since Daniel perspires
with a faint sickly odor. Amelia quickly bites her lip, but
Daniel takes no notice, seems totally unaware of his turbulent
body. She turns the pages of his dog-eared book, past the E
Major that is torturing him with its hateful staccato. He draws
back sharply, then hunches forward, a blend of courtesy,
apology, misery; he seems to hope his carefully controlled
breathing will help her turn the pages.

Daniel is taller than Amelia and only a bit younger, a
shameful state for him to endure, but somehow necessary. He
could have chosen an older piano teacher. He has told Amelia
this would have been an evasion of reality. It is better for him
to confront his true condition—his maturity and his igno-
rance—head on. He is a senior in chemistry, had no opportunity to study music as a child, studies furiously now, sets
impossible goals for himself.

Amelia turns to the gentle C Sharp Minor. "Do the scale first
in two octaves, please, as a warm-up." Daniel falls eagerly
onto the keyboard. "Now the principal chords in arpeggios."
He obeys ferociously. She is preparing him to sightread the
waltz. It is a gratuitous gesture, for Daniel has already played
all of the waltzes in his book, again and again. He has made
this music a fetish, his private war. He refuses to be led in a
different direction. Amelia has offered him Kabalevsky. He
found it trivial. Schumann was sentimental, Bach mechanical,
Mozart frivolous. "Now the waltz." He plays competently
through the chromatics of the first page then stumbles at the
piu mosso, unable to pick up the tempo. "You must start each
phrase with the fourth finger and cross only once, Daniel.

Then it is perfectly logical to play six notes with five fingers."
He begins again earnestly, but after only four measures the
third finger creeps back to start each group of eighth notes.
"Stop, please. Why don't you trust the strength of your fourth
and fifth fingers?" Amelia couches this question in a canny,
conspiratorial tone. They are detectives sorting over puzzling
evidence, surgeons parting hot flesh in search of a festering
sore. She wonders if Daniel, with his heightened sensibilities,
finds all of this totally absurd.

But he only continues to study his hands intently. "I exercise my fingers constantly."

"Of course you do, but you do not let them do their work.
You must train your instincts as well as your fingers."

"I'm sorry."

"You needn't be sorry. You need only to trust your fingers, all
of them." This teacher's mind of Amelia's is as cold and objec-
tive as a machine, a computer that plays over data searching
for aberrations, splits meaning and motion and realigns them
deftly. "You are picturing the release in your mind, trying to get
the fingers off the keys as quickly as possible. That is wrong.
You must focus on the attack, sense how the finger reaches out
and grasps the key. Then finger memory, muscle memory will
take charge." She wonders why Daniel tolerates such pre-
ciosity, why he does not suddenly sneer and strike her.

But he participates in these fanciful ventures without question. He nods, whips a pencil from his pocket and writes "grasp
and attack" on the score, considers, then underlines the words
heavily.

His intensity suddenly becomes unbearable to Amelia, in-
spires its opposite in her. She turns the page to the D-flat
minor section with a sense of complete detachment. Daniel
plays it majestically, heavily, sonorously, lethargically, with all
of the accidentals perfectly in place. "That's very nice, Daniel."

He nods, then suddenly, viciously, strikes the keyboard. "No,
it's not! It's not nice! Excuse me, but it's not nice. I have ears. I
can hear. No one needs to tell me." He looks into Amelia's face

and then past it into some vast, arid place whose landscape is known only to him. "Professor Perlingiero, this isn't any of my business and perhaps I shouldn't ask, but I need to know something."

"What is it you need to know, Daniel?"

"When your baby died. When. . . . Did it make you a better artist? I haven't suffered. I've never suffered, Professor Perlingiero."

Amelia feels an instant's sharp surprise, but it passes quickly, and it then seems to her she has known for some time that Daniel would ask her this, that she woke this morning hearing the question like rain against the window, the next step in some inevitable pattern.

He drives on relentlessly. "The answer could be as simple as that, and I've failed to grasp it because it's so obvious."

Daniel's juxtaposition of a Chopin waltz and her dead son strikes Amelia as an act of enormous invention, of artistic creation and, like all good art, it has about it a strange inevitability. She thinks of Daniel in his room beside his record player, the flow of sound washing over him, transporting him, provoking him to define shapes like this one in his mind. "I see no point in suffering, Daniel."

"I'm sorry. I'm so sorry. Forgive me, please."

"It's all right."

"The fourth and fifth fingers?"

"I think so."

He smiles, a little wan, a little sick, and enters into some impossible pact with himself. He gathers his music and manages, incredibly, to walk directly into the piano bench.

"Good-bye, Daniel. Have a good week. Good luck."

He is replaced in the doorway by a smiling Mrs. Mills. "That boy plays so beautifully. You can't know how much I enjoy it here, having the music to listen to all day. It's so much nicer than when I worked in the geography department, although the people there were very nice. I would never say a word against the people, but having the music to listen to is like being paid a bonus." These remarks are a small gift she offers. Then more quietly, "Your husband called to say he'll pick you up at four."

"Thank you, Mrs. Mills."

"He's concerned about you. I told him you were fine, that you and your student were playing lovely music, that everything was fine." She raises her hands tentatively, flutters them. It seems this conversation is not precisely what she had hoped for and she is uncertain what to say next.

"I'm glad you like the music," says Amelia. It is as much help as she can offer. The rest of the world does not exist, has never existed, except for Daniel, Mrs. Mills, and herself. The three of them have dreamed all of the world's great cities, written all of its symphonies, conceived and born a million children who no longer exist except as dust motes hanging above the melody line of a Chopin waltz. So much is behind them, accomplished, abandoned. There is nothing left for them now except to discuss the geography department.

At this moment, and into these mad imaginings, Mrs. Mills suddenly opens her heart to Amelia. "A woman's wise if she has more than one thing in her life. We're all hostages to fate . . . but you have music. No one can take that from you. I remember my great-grandmother. She was against music. She thought it was frivolity and the work of the devil." Mrs. Mills considers and seems to wish this had come out differently. "Isn't that a curiosity? That she would think that? It was pure superstition. But you have music. That's a real blessing."

Amelia feels swift resentment at this intrusion. "I expect my husband and I will have other children." Her tone rebukes Mrs. Mills. "Our son lived four days. It does not seem an adequate length for a life, does it? And he wanted very much to live. He struggled."

Quick tears spring to Mrs. Mills's eyes. "I only wanted to say. . . ." But she does not know what she wants to say.

Amelia's next student has come in, observes this interchange discreetly and from a distance. Julie, a petulant, antagonistic girl, a voice major with a deficiency in piano that must be cleared this semester if she is to graduate. A mezzo-soprano with a taste for show tunes.

"Come in, Julie."

The girl arranges herself at the piano slowly, meticulously, to fill the time; she opens her book of easy classics to Mozart's "Turkish March" and stares at it wearily. She sings at night with a dance band and never gets enough sleep, is always preoccupied. She begins sluggishly, making no attempt to play at tempo, and does not bother to shift the left-hand chord when the harmony changes.

"Let's look at the left hand, Julie," says Amelia. "At the *sforzando* the third expands to a fourth. Do you see it?" Julie peers at the score and pretends this is new, fascinating information to her. Amelia presses gently. "Your ear is quite good. You should be able to hear the pattern when the harmony shifts. I believe all you need to do is focus in, listen more closely as you play."

But the girl has lost all interest in the point Amelia is making. "Why does it go to three sharps?" she asks. "Why doesn't it stay in C?"

"It's the Rondo of the A-Major Sonata. Most of the sonata is in three sharps. What you are playing is only an excerpt. The key is not C but A minor."

"Singers can't read music," Julie offers wearily. "Everyone knows that."

"An inability to read will not make you a better singer," Amelia says sharply, her annoyance growing.

But Julie finds this remark enormously funny and laughs over it in a leisurely way. She opens her purse and locates a tissue, wipes imagined perspiration from the palms of her hands, sends Amelia a sly glance. All of this seems meant to say there are great areas of experience in which Julie is fully competent: bright rooms, sunny landscapes, coteries of brilliant minds to which Amelia with her three sharps and expanding chords can never be admitted.

"Play the right hand alone, please, Julie. Those are six-teenth notes. You must try to take them faster. Play with the fingers, not the hand. The smallest muscular unit is the most flexible." Julie begins, falters, stops. Amelia looks at her own right hand, at the fragile blue veins lying quietly in the crease of her arm, as if she had no pulse. "Please turn to the little Bach prelude," she tells Julie. It is the first piece in the book but Julie pretends she cannot find it, turns the pages with soft, tired fingers, feigns interest in each passing title, pushes Amelia past endurance. "Julie, you will have to prepare three pieces from this book, play them from memory and at tempo, or I will not pass you."

The girl gives her a scathing, sidelong look, plays the Bach limply, leaves without a good-bye.

The afternoon passes until Mrs. Mills tells Amelia that her last student has cancelled. Amelia finds Vladimir Ashkenazy's recording of Chopin waltzes, sets it on the turntable, stares entranced at the pianist's photograph on the record cover as the D Flat Major begins. Dark, professional eyes stare back at her. The photographer has made Ashkenazy's face the color of pale apricots, repeated the hue in the boards of the stage beneath his feet, splashed it in shadows across the legs of the ebony black piano, let one provocative stripe of color reach out and touch the reproduction of a British flag and the leg-end, "Imported from England." A dingy label announces, "Record Department. Price Reduced. Plus Tax." The opus numbers for six mazurkas and a barcarolle sit in a neat column under the title: "Side Two."

Ashkenazy completes the first waltz, falls silent, then begins the C Sharp Minor, reaching into the eighth notes confidently, as if to assure Amelia. Then he hurries on into the A Flat Major, a bit bored yet seemingly aware of this afternoon's strange necessities. As if, thinks Amelia, he knows he will not get his supper until he pulls all of the absurdities of this album cover into a unified whole. He must make the Union Jack come down from its corner and dance lightly across the white keys, restore dignity to the shabby, cut-rate price seal.

Amelia stops him and turns the record over, suddenly needing to hear the somber, less-spirited mazurkas. Ashkenazy hardly pedals them at all, choosing instead to connect the notes with finger legato. Doing it the hard way. He senses that Amelia is following his pedaling, and a small, wry smile lights the face in the photograph. "If you pedaled the legato . . . ?" Amelia begins, musing, and is unable to finish the question.

He seems to understand and the eyes in the photograph lighten with amusement.

Amelia does not share this amusement, and sharp, perhaps unreasonable anger sets free the difficult words. "If you pedaled the legato rather than fingering it . . . would you die? Would you or would you not die?"

Ashkenazy's face twitches with surprise. "Oh, that!" he says, and Amelia wonders what on earth he has expected her to ask. "That would be absurd, wouldn't it?" Recording in England, he has picked up or is effecting a British accent and British mannerisms. He ends his statements with little questions. "Death is perfectly absurd, don't you think?"

Amelia is not completely convinced. "You don't believe in contingencies?"

"No." He's quite certain about it. He is a good teacher, inspiring confidence, finding hope everywhere.

"Chopin was a little mad," says Amelia. Like Daniel, she wants to be sure nothing has been overlooked.

But Ashkenazy scoffs at Chopin's alleged madness. "He was merely a bit childlike. Once he threw a tantrum when George Sand gave the choicest piece of chicken to her son instead of to him."

She has not expected him to recall an episode involving a child. "I can understand that," she says. "Anyone could, of course, but Mr. Ashkenazy . . . I have never played really well."

"Neither have I!" says Ashkenazy. He sighs, grasps now what she is trying to say, then moves into the barcarolle that will finish out the side.

"I hope you understand about Daniel," says Amelia.

Ashkenazy says he doesn't mind Daniel at all, "but be charitable to Mrs. Mills," he adds.

"I have always meant to be."

"Music frightens Mrs. Mills," says Ashkenazy, "frightens her terribly, stirs her up, don't you know?"

Amelia is surprised he knows Mrs. Mills this well, but of course he travels, meets scores of people, could know anyone, anyone at all. "That's a good way of putting it," she answers, "but Mrs. Mills loves music. I really believe her when she says she loves music."

"Of course!" says Ashkenazy. "Your husband is here. I just saw him drive into the parking lot from my window."

It is Mrs. Mills speaking. She has quietly opened the door and come in. "He looks fine."

"Yes, we're both fine. Very fine."

"Mrs. Perlingiero . . . Amelia . . . I hope you didn't mind our girl talk."

Amelia slips the record back into its jacket and sees that Ashkenazy is still watching, waiting, growing a bit impatient. She takes a breath and reaches for Mrs. Mills's hand. The two women resemble neighbors settling some small dispute. It is not a handshake; it is little more than a clumsy gesture, but Ashkenazy is satisfied. "Work on it," he says in his clipped British accent, already centered on his next student.

Mrs. Mills steers Amelia gently into the hall, reaches behind her to close and lock the door. Without Mrs. Mills's permission, no one will enter Amelia's office, play her piano, sit at her desk, browse through her unruly piles of music, look out of her window. Mrs. Mills turns the doorknob one last time to be sure, taps Amelia's namecard firmly down into its brass frame. From all of life's possibilities, thinks Amelia, these things have been abstracted and arranged. Mrs. Mills, Ashkenazy, and Amelia have them in their charge. "Have a nice evening, Mrs. Mills."

"You too."

In the front hall, the orchestra room stands empty, its doors propped open. Chairs and music stands are clustered in an abandoned tangle. Someone has collected all of the scores; they sit in a neat stack on the table at the front of the room, twenty-five or thirty fragments that, when assembled, can produce a Viennese waltz, a bold proposal from the brain of Johann Strauss. A janitor has thrown open the windows, pulled a bulky floor-polishing machine into the room. It sits importantly, its heavy cord still hanked, ready to perform. An early evening breeze finds the open windows, slips in past the chairs, plays suggestively with the sheets of music on the front table.

In the Music Library

*I*can't tell you how much I like soft bags that zipper open
and shut with articulate little growls, snap with subtle
clicks, or pucker voluptuously around drawstrings: purses,
knapsacks, haversacks, school satchels, beach bags, bikers'
packs, High Sierra survival bags, rucksacks, weekend organiz-
ers, duffel bags. My favorites are the soft, shapeless ones that
immediately assume the contour of any objects placed in
them: stenographers' notebooks, cameras with or without
zoom lenses, copies of the *Portable Walt Whitman,* cans
of pork and beans with pull tops, sweat shirts crumpled
into sensuous knots of sweaty cotton-polyester, wooden re-
corders imported from Germany, rolled copies of the *Minneapolis Tribune,* navel oranges, pocket calculators, high-heeled
pumps, Schirmer editions of the *Well-Tempered Clavier.*

Each of the functional objects that support daily life
assumes significance, dynamic potential, when carried in a
soft bag, like a brilliant and highly technical cadenza you wait
for, knowing every note in advance, yet waiting, a small knot
of delectable fear in the throat, to be lifted out of ordinary
sensibility.

Whenever I enter department stores, I go immediately to
purses, bags, and luggage to examine the inventory. I send
zippers flying wildly back and forth, peer into tissue-filled
cavities, and attempt to see each dark, inviting space as a
thing-in-itself designed purposefully to contain a given object, and also as a great unformed opportunity to lend itself to

any chance rattail comb or disassembled clarinet that might appear on the horizon. I want, of course, to happen someday upon a bag that will accommodate my entire body. Something like a cello bag is how I picture it, a marvelous outer skin that will immediately transform me into an object at once mysterious and knowable. Indulging this fantasy is, I think, no more self-destructive than sky diving, doing latch hook rugs, sprouting alfalfa seeds, suing for whiplash, or playing the sitar.

I am thinking about these soft, shapeless bags when I ask Felix, "What is the name of the disease where you feel responsible for all of the evil in the world?" But just then Marge Kochnik comes into the music library late for work and screaming she got the job as ballet accompanist. She is screaming this at me and at the shelf of new arrivals behind me, at the work table with the pot of glue where she is supposed to be right now gluing the pockets into the new arrivals, and at the IBM Selectric where she is supposed to be right now typing the cards to go into the pockets. Then she looks at Felix and decides to stop screaming. In a resonant contralto voice with an unpredictable tessitura she says, "I am resigning from the staff of the university music library immediately because I have to practice." It's the money, she tells Felix, and nothing personal. A simple case of economics. As she puts this coda on her statement her voice quavers.

Marge is tall, all muscle and knobby joints. I look at her across the stack of records I am cataloging and wonder why she has chosen to be a musician when she could be the best professional volleyball player in the game.

Her eyes meet mine and exuberance bursts from her once more. This is appropriate. Although I am not officially a dancer, I have certain attributes that qualify me as an authority on dance. "Aida!" she cries. A single lunge brings her to my side. She pulls me to my feet in a cool, neat athletic gesture and shouts, "Wish me luck!" She cups my skinny, black shoulders between her mammoth palms as if I am a basketball about to be hefted spinning into the air. I refuse to smile. I am not finished thinking about soft bags and disease descriptions that organize my free-floating anxieties into categories. There is an orderly correlative between zipper bags and diseases, and this morning I am quite near its discovery. But I am not to be left to reflection. I am danced about the office of the music library like a rag doll.

"I told them I was a proficient improviser!" Marge howls. She is stricken with fear at this thought but she does not stop bouncing me around my desk. "Do you think I can do it?"

Felix Marconi whom everyone calls Felix Macaroni has been preparing himself to be very angry but now changes his mind and decides to be knowledgeable instead. He sits back in his head-librarian chair and screws up his eyes and then his mouth. "Stay with the natural minor, Marge," he says, pale as a mushroom, anemic, blue-veined, manicured, twitchy, allergic. He is thirty-four years old and his narrow shoulders can barely carry the weight of his estimation of himself. He believes he is sincere, erudite, shrewd, encyclopedic. He thinks he looks like someone who would speak only German. "Just stay with the natural minor, Marge-girl, and you'll be okay. You'll be absolutely o-kay-ke-doke." Felix grew up in Redkey, Indiana, far from the sophistication of Minneapolis. In Redkey, presumably, folks say things like "o-kay-ke-doke."

Marge deposits me in a corner beside a poster announcing a Gershwin concert and begins scratching various parts of her body enthusiastically, a no-nonsense digging into her mesomorphic flesh.

I do not speak nor alter my expression. I believe I am the only black woman in the world named Aida Williamson. I am certainly the only student in the school of music named Aida. My thin, black, surly, overdressed presence is regarded with respect. I am totemic, charismatic, magical, sullen. I also play cello moderately well and am majoring in performance on the premise that shortly every major symphony in the country will be required to hire one black female cellist. Managers will bid for my services with all the lust and greed now lavished on promising quarterbacks. I can also, when required, double on flute. I can also, when required, dance, and I am in demand at those functions where people express themselves in unstructured ways.

At present I am, essentially, a witch. A black woman named Aida in the music department really has no other option. I am a communal good luck charm, a black Blarney stone, a Chaucerian pigges bone, a shimmering, high yellow mustard seed. I am touched, patted, stroked, fawned upon. I carry spiritual responsibility for the school of music, something in the manner of a royal Romanian government in exile.

Although a bit insular, my existence isn't all that bad. I sew myself orange capes and lavender wraparound skirts, order overpowering floral perfumes from a drugstore in Port-au-Prince, subsist on a diet of tacos and candy bars, read Borges whose responsibilities are similar to mine, play chamber music with a group that calls itself, absurdly, the Baroque-Aires with two capitals. In the controversy over the Haydn revival, I come down in the negative.

I do not espouse Suzuki, play Charles Ives due to certain technical difficulties, sing gospel music, talk about my brother who is a patent attorney in St. Paul. I believe I am arrogant in exactly the correct ratio to my position, considering that I am supposed to burn with repressed feelings and have roots.

Actually, I like Marge Kochnik a lot. I also like Felix and this wilderness of love, the music library. In accordance with all of this, I now straighten my clothing with the slow, graceful (I fancy) gestures I have always associated with the word *negress*, and return to my desk.

Marge says once again that she must leave her library job immediately, and Felix Macaroni, whose spiritual dimension does not go beyond marveling from time to time that his initials perfectly match those of *frequency modulation*, decides that he will, after all, become angry. He frets, sweats, farts delicately, and turns petulant. "I can't replace you in a day," he tells Marge importantly. "You are letting us all down rather badly, Marge-girl, rather badly." It is a lie. Half of the students in the music department are out of work and will take a job with Felix on ten minutes notice. But Felix believes his own lies. To replace Marge, he will solicit a dozen resumes and study them with great cunning for two weeks. He will then select an advanced music student, cast him/her as ignoble apprentice, and spend an additional week explaining (to her/him) the difference between a capo and *de capo*. Felix Macaroni sees his music library as a cell of organized enlightenment in a world of screaming disorder, a bastion constantly endangered by people who scratch expensive recordings, rip aria pages from libretto books, write *Seig Heil!* in German language editions, draw genitalia on magazine photographs of Beverly Sills, fondle one another in the listening carrels. Human failing is his daily burden. It edges into his daydreams like a wet, creeping stain and spoils his courage. It feeds his most primitive fears and erodes all of his hope into peevishness. All of these things appear now as small signs in the luminous aura about his head, a neon circle of fifths he sets flashing off and on to intimidate Marge Kochnik.

"It's lunch hour!" Marge cries suddenly with a thrill of discovery, miraculously delivered from all this torment by the authority of the clock. She fears Felix terribly. She believes he holds subtle but extensive authority throughout the university and can influence, by whim, grades in advanced harmony, distribution of dormitory rooms, orchestra assignments, the balance of power in the Middle East. Challenging him has cost her a great price; she is white about the eyes. But, buoyed up by the sovereignty of the clock and the proximity of my splendid presence, she is emboldened and courageous. "You can dance for me, Aida! We can practice on your lunch hour!" She grips my hand cruelly and marches me out of the library. To keep pace with her I hop, skip, jump, sarabande, mazurka, and gigue.

"Let them eat lunch!" Felix calls after us truculently, Gounod's Mephistopheles confident in the certainty of our eventual destruction. "Let them eat cake! Let them eat their hearts out!"

Marge harrumphs me around corners, down halls, and into an empty dance studio, a thin, gaudy, black Pooh Bear trailed behind an aging Christopher Robin.

Set free, I breathe in deeply through my nostrils, a canny, winded hound scenting its environs, and behold myself in the floor-to-ceiling mirrored wall. The barre slices my image neatly in half and I fantasize that my upper torso, dislodged, will suddenly tumble forward and plummet onto the floor with a dull, gray thud while my left leg, still holding firm to my lower body, will begin to rise slowly and move into a stunning pirouette, a half-butterfly opening into sunlight.

Marge raises the lid of the grand piano, stares hungrily at a pile of music on the floor, picks up half a dozen scores, and hugs them in her powerful arms. The truth is Marge cannot improvise at all: not in the natural minor, the harmonic minor, nor the melodic minor; not in the Ionian, Aeolian, Dorian, Phrygian, Lydian, nor Mixolydian mode; not in the treble, bass, tenor, alto, soprano, nor the movable C clef; not at *largo, grave, lento, adagio, andante,* nor *presto.*

What Marge can do is discover a frail melody line with her right hand and supplement it with four chords in her left hand: a tonic in root position, a sub dominant in root position, a dominant in root position, and a bastard seventh in a variety of positions. I go to her and gently pry loose the music she is clutching. "Yes," she groans, "I must improvise."

I remove my sandals and stand barefoot at the barre, raising one leg and then the other, my lavender skirt draping to left and then to right like a Japanese fan that has forgotten how to open. I close my eyes and concentrate, trying to forget everything I learned in Miss Goodwin's Ballet School in St.

70

Paul. After all, I am African, I am filled with residues of racial memory, I am hostile, I have rhythm.

Marge strikes the keys violently and lurches into a precarious version of the "Poet and Peasant Overture." Degraded, I refuse to move. She considers and modulates into "Embraceable You" but the accidentals are too challenging and she abandons it for the pure harmonies of "Amazing Grace." I cross my arms and sigh. "Dammit!" Marge cries. "Why can't you dance?" Desperately, she does an inverted jump shot at the pile of music and whips the score for *Coppélia* onto the music rack. "Amazing Grace" spins off crazily into a serenade-like waltz passage.

"I am not Coppélia!" I cry wickedly. "A dumb-ass mechanical doll!"

Terror now clutches Marge Kochnik and sends a frantic appeal that plunges into her gut. There is only one thing Marge does well at the piano. Since the age of fourteen, performing in student recitals in South Minneapolis, she has made a specialty of playing Wagner reductions. Now, eyes burning, she sweeps *Coppélia* from the piano and begins from memory a dark, rumbling rendition of the "Magic Fire Music."

I relinquish the barre, lift my arms, wish briefly that I had read Alex Haley, send myself sailing into the center of the room in two wobbly leaps, and settle into a poorly executed drop that scrapes the skin off my left ankle. I murmur a brief obscenity and bring the palms of my hands together under my chin, modest as a pilgrim, then raise them slowly in mute salute. Marge slaps the keyboard, confident that sheer volume will reproduce all of the nuances of Eugene Ormandy and the Philadelphia Orchestra. Her cloying minor apes the cellos in a fierce bass clef legato and I leap recklessly. Brasses and basses rumble to life under her broad palms and, against my will, the music's dark mythology invades my body.

Marge pauses to let the basses fade, preparatory to bringing in a cacophony of glockenspiels, and in that tremulous moment of silence, in my last instant of sanity, I call over to her, "You'll be okay, Marge! The dancers can't dance either! No one will suspect you're a fake!"

Grateful for this benediction, she lowers her eyes, swells with virtuosity, raises her hands above her head, and hurls them like thunderbolts down upon the keyboard. An orgy of bells explodes and splatters upon every surface of the studio. Dings and dongs ricochet and careen wildly about the room like frenzied fireflies. Where each lands, a tiny tongue of flame leaps up. A spray of sparks nips sharply at my skinned ankle. I cry out angrily and my voice is swallowed up in a howl of violas.

Marge sees my pain, misunderstands, grins broadly, breathes smoke from her nostrils and, in an all-or-nothing drive for the goal, strikes Promethean chords that shape fierce, primal trumpets. I leap about frantically trying to stamp out the spreading flames that lick at my skirt and begin to form an inexorable ring about me. But it is too late. From the choking fire rises the form of a scowling African warrior carrying a brightly colored spear that he shakes ominously at me. I feel my lungs bursting with stinging smoke and know I am responsible for all of the evil in the world. Music and fire lash pitilessly, Marge pounds relentlessly, I dance helplessly.

Marge Kochnik is breathless before this majestic display of her virtuosity. My skinny black body whipping and flapping about so recklessly confirms her existence, defines her identity, gives her an extra shot at the free-throw line. A shriek of pain breaks from my lips but Marge will not be hurried. She lets the screaming violins return and fade again and again, like Simon and Garfunkel tormenting a plagal cadence into resolution. And only when I have been tormented past all endurance does she finally bring in the glittering song of the French horn to rain down and extinguish the fire. Then, seconds before the final whistle, Marge Kochnik zippers me shut with a full-throated Wagnerian growl, an exhausted cello swallowed up into the dark sanctuary of a perfectly contoured bag. I settle into a lopsided swoon and the soot drops from me as Marge's last harmonic echoes seep off into the cracks of the floor. Then, rising slowly, I lift one arm in regal salute. "Go!" I cry. "Go, Marge Kochnik, and bullshit the dance department!"

She genuflects and lopes off down the hall, not wishing to miss her lunch at the dorm since it is already paid for and they serve until one-thirty.

I smooth the folds of my skirt over my abdomen, consider the eerie, dark potential of my womb, and discover that my stomach is growling. Retrieving my sandals, I inspect my bruised ankle and head for the candy bar machine. Then, with a full and generous heart, I decide to buy two candy bars, one for my friend, parsimonious, protracted, pissed-off Felix Macaroni.

A Hidden Thing

This was years ago. My Aunt Bonnie was my mother's younger sister, so young I didn't have to call her aunt. Mother said, "Before I had you, Bonnie was my little girl." The words made me think of walking through grass and finding something, perhaps a bird's egg. The three of us were strong together—Mother, Bonnie, and I—like all the parts of a project in place. I could imagine someone with a long pointer explaining us to an audience, or a person in another room listening carefully to our conversation, even when the chatter was all in fun. Mother had other family but they were miles away, mostly living on farms.

Bonnie was nineteen the year she got sick; I was fourteen. It was the year I memorized a nine-page story called "The Little Match Girl" in two days. This was for a school program. Another girl had gotten sick and the teacher had given the piece to me. Two days. I hadn't known I was capable of such a feat, and I wondered if that was how life happened, finding a talent one day and building a life around it.

Bonnie was pretty, fair like the Steeds on my grandfather's side, quick to speak up and mostly cheerful, but always living at the edge of something, inclined to turn simple words into swift argument without warning, to stride off on concerns big or small, real or imagined, then to let everything dissolve into warm reconciliation. My father called the Steeds fearless. He said people like that could do a lot, but he hoped they were never put in charge of running the entire world.

Mother and I were like the Porters on the other side, darker in coloring and more reserved. The differences between Steeds and Porters were really more subtle than they seem with the telling. Only my father found them significant.

One of the largest employers in our small city was a garment factory. In it, Bonnie spent her days sewing sleeves into men's shirts, sewing on pockets. I never saw the inside of the factory. They didn't take school groups to tour industry then; they didn't have career counseling. We never thought about it.

Bonnie's shift started early and finished at four in the afternoon. Sometimes after school I waited for her to come out, standing on the street corner across from the railroad yard. The garment workers were mostly girls. The ones who didn't have cars came out a side door and walked across the tracks, a shortcut to the bus stop and the street back into town. They came out looking distracted, like people interrupted in the middle of something. They peered left and right and blinked into the afternoon sun as if distance were a concept that had to be relearned every day. Behind them, the low brown hum of the plant never ceased.

Once when I was very small my parents took me to the spring musical at the high school. I always remembered it because we came home so late that night and I fell asleep in an instant. Usually I had trouble going to sleep, even as a small child. In the grand finale of the musical all the girls came on stage and sang, "Reuben, Reuben, I've been thinking,/What a grand world this would be/If the men were all transported/Far beyond the Northern Sea." Then the boys joined them and sang it with "Rachel" and "girls" in the lyric. I knew the song. We all did. After they sang, the students moved through intricate patterns a little like a square dance, while the music played. The girls' full skirts whirled as they made their turns, and the boys looked as if they were doing exercises with their good clothes on. My father said someone really drilled the students to put that together. Anyone might naturally sing, but dancing was harder. He called it dancing, and said it wasn't a natural thing people did easily.

But Father was wrong. Bonnie always moved like someone dancing, especially when she came out after work. The other girls would stumble over the tracks and rutted ground as if the sun had robbed them of coordination as well as sight, but Bonnie could pick a path and never falter. She crossed the rails by setting her feet neatly on the ties, never seeming to look down, even when she was wearing high heels. She would give her skirt the slightest touch with one hand and it would dance free of her legs as she stepped over the tracks. I couldn't do it, even with practice.

When Bonnie put on lipstick in a restaurant she picked up a tableknife and used the side of the shiny blade as a mirror. To spread the lipstick, she moved the inner casing of the tube across her lips in swift strokes. This inner rim always bore the imprint of her mouth, like a fingerprint or the mark of a kiss on a Valentine. She often took me to restaurants after work. Usually, we ate donuts; sometimes we ate pieces of pie. When she paid the check Bonnie said to me, "My treat. I'm working." I loved the words, the suggestion that I was not actually a child but a person out of work, someone who would be getting a job any day and paying my share of the donut checks. Leaving a restaurant with Bonnie, walking off along the sidewalk into the waning day, I would experience a delicious sadness which I took to be a glimpse of adult responsibility. Then I would imagine I was walking with an object balanced on my head, a book perhaps. I would tell myself my total future depended on going a certain distance without dropping it.

Bonnie didn't sew but she altered clothes after she bought them. Mother said, "She's done that for as long as I can remember." Once Bonnie bought a soft red dress, took off the belt of the same material, and substituted one made of fur. It would have been wrong on anyone else. "You know you're too plump for that," Mother said. When Bonnie cinched in the belt, a little roll of flesh appeared above it. Both mother and I were thin and straight as winter sticks. "You should wear shirtwaist dresses with a fuller bodice and a self-belt," said Mother, "a single color." With new clothes, we always recited the rules of correct dress, as if assuring some invisible committee on fashion we knew what was expected of us. Then Bonnie attached fur pompons to the ends of the original belt, threaded it under her collar, and looped it into a necktie. Everything came together perfectly; the dress was a costume. The three of us fell into laughter, and I longed to have a small roll of flesh around my scrawny middle.

Bonnie had trouble managing her paycheck. She'd put a coat on layaway and then spend the money needed to get it out on a pair of shoes. Sometimes she forgot entirely to pay bills. Everything came right in the end; she'd borrow from my mother, ten dollars here and twenty there. She always repaid the loans but her constant frenzy over money made me grow up thinking life was more hazardous than it actually was.

My father had learned not to criticize Bonnie. Mother wouldn't stand for it. He directed all of his ideas at me, not as criticism but as moralizing. "Patty, a girl is foolish to put every dollar she earns on her back." He told me this as he hoed the green onions in our backyard garden, or tinkered on the car, when Mother wasn't around. He meant Bonnie, of course.

I never knew if my father had wanted a son, or even additional children. I measure his goodness by that. He was a carpenter. I could walk along the street and point to houses where he'd worked, building in closets, remodeling kitchens, finishing off attics into bedrooms. Sometimes when there was no school, my mother would make him a hot lunch to eat on the job, instead of the brown-bag lunch he usually carried. I would take the plate of food to him, wrapped in newspapers to hold the heat. He would be working when I arrived, kneeling above his hammer, perhaps standing on a ladder to fit molding over a high door, his face set to the rhythm and shape of the task. Only once growing up did I ever think of my father as a fellow human being. This was on a day when I had carried him his food. I found him planing a board, the curls of aromatic wood dancing from the blade, fluttering to the floor as endless and numberless as snowflakes, forming across the years a small mountain. *How can he stand it?* I thought with a fear so sharp it seemed the floor had tilted under me, but the moment passed in an instant, a pain too great to consider.

The smile he always gave me when I handed him his food held that special courtesy reserved for women and girls. I took it as my right. Not until I had a son of my own would it occur to me how splendid my father's life might have been with a boy beside him.

But he was a man who asked and expected little. Whatever his original feelings about a daughter, they'd been smoothly shaped into graceful love by the time I was old enough to perceive them. Hoeing his onions, he said to me, "The world is bigger than this town, bigger than men's shirts." I don't think he knew what a girl might do anymore than I did, but he wanted me to think about it.

His greatest fear was that I would marry too soon. "I'm not against marriage," he labored to explain, "but if a girl marries too young she short-circuits her future." I have no idea where the term *short-circuit* had come from, but he seemed to find it totally descriptive and used it again and again.

One of his ideas was for me to go off to college and come back a schoolteacher. "In a college dormitory you live as if you were in a fine hotel," he told me. "You have your meals in a dining room. Sometimes they have teas, with lemon slices and sugar cubes for the tea, and someone playing on a grand piano. You meet people from other places and they talk about books and fine paintings." Where had the wealth of detail come from? At fourteen, I gave him little cause for hope, responding mostly with docile silence.

My own inner life was seldom career-oriented. Sometimes I wondered what became of all the shirts made in the garment factory, boxes of shirts, truckloads of shirts. It occurred to me their production might actually be a mistake, the result of a terrible misunderstanding. Perhaps in some distant city—I pictured a shabby street beside an ocean, a place where large ships lay—tons of shirts were piling up, unused and unwanted. Sometimes it seemed I was the only person in the world who knew about this, and it was my responsibility to dispose of the shirts with a swift and cunning solution. I wouldn't tell Bonnie what I was doing; in some way that was built into the situation. Nobility and self-sacrifice were involved.

Bonnie had her own apartment but she came by our house nearly every day. She liked my mother to wash and set her hair. Her own apartment had only a shower and she liked to use our tub. Often, Bonnie and I took baths together, washing each other's backs, sometimes splashing as riotously as small children. I marveled at the roundness of her creamy body, her full, slightly pendulous breasts. Bonnie bought me creams to rub on my own hopeless chest; she gave me a bra too large for me and we spent an hour arranging soft handkerchiefs to fill the cups in convincing fashion. Mother said, "Now I want to pay you for the bra, Bonnie. You're always buying Patty things out of your own pocket."

And Bonnie said, "Jean, you are the silliest person! Just see how sweet she looks. Don't you think that's payment enough?"

If Bonnie had gone on a date with a boy the night before, she always told us about it. Any man who wasn't married was a boy, at least for years and until he grew old. Bonnie told us everything. If she'd been to a movie we heard not just the story of it but what she'd worn, whom she'd seen, and the full menu if she'd been taken to eat. Long before I kissed a boy, I knew exactly what to expect. Some kissed with their lips tightly closed which meant a cold nature, but a boy's mouth full-open was pushy and disgusting. The ideal was something in between, and Bonnie was against tongues, from start to finish.

If a boy had been forward to her sister, Mother would flush with anger as if her own body had been trespassed. "You stand up for yourself!" she would order.

And Bonnie would cry, "Honestly! What do you *think* I do?"

Then Mother full of pride would say, "If these boys only knew how you talk about them!"

Most of the time I can't remember weather. The pictures I see are framed with interior space. My father had built our house himself, putting in many gracious appointments usually found only in the homes of the wealthy, and including features that were ahead of the times. He could buy wholesale and do the work himself. Overall, the house was a modest bungalow, but there were French doors between the living room and the dining room, each small rectangle of glass set in hand-finished walnut. There was a den paneled in cherry wood. Long before such things were common, our kitchen had a dishwasher, a phone with a shoulder rest so my mother could talk to friends while cooking.

Our hall phone sat on a recessed shelf, with an additional shelf for phone books. I have always associated the hall telephone with calls to the dentist. Nature had not blessed me with strong teeth. My entire childhood can be viewed as a constantly evolving strategy to save my mouth from ruin. I seemed to have no natural defense against decay, chipping, red and swollen gums. My teeth grew at erratic angles and developed in eccentric patterns. Treatment usually involved pain. All of the discomfort, I was told, was in the service of the fine mouth I would someday have. I lacked the courage to embrace this view and lived day-to-day, grateful for any month that passed without phone calls to and from the dentist, without visits to his office. For me, dental pain was a gestalt that included the curious way the dentist's graying hair curled just above his ears, the rattle of car keys as my mother prepared to drive me to appointments, and the hall telephone that often brought results—almost always bad news—of tests and X-rays.

Bonnie was at home in her own shower when she discovered the lump in her breast; she telephoned my mother. "Ninety percent of lumps are harmless," Mother said at once. For a long time it seemed to me our lives might have been very different if Mother had answered on the kitchen phone, an instrument I associated with pleasant conversation, but we were passing through the hall when the call came, carrying fresh sheets to the bedrooms. "Ninety-nine percent are harmless, Bonnie. *Ninety-nine!*" Mother had turned white. She switched the phone to her left hand; with her right she opened the phone book. I think she had planned to look up our doctor's number; then she seemed to change her mind, and began simply to turn the pages of the book. "No, don't come here," she ordered. "Go directly to Dr. Horn's office. We'll meet you there."

Young as I was, I understood the conversation completely. "It's Saturday," I said. "Only Dr. Graham is in on Saturday."

"Go to Dr. Graham's," Mother told Bonnie. "It's Saturday." Bonnie's apartment was downtown, an easy walk to either office.

I'm not sure we even remembered to tell Father we were leaving. As we shot out of the driveway, Mother shifting gears frantically, I said, "Dr. Graham is old. He's had years and years of experience. That's very important in making a diagnosis. What you're buying in a case like this is the doctor's judgment." I did not know where the words had come from.

"He's the only doctor left with any humanity," said Mother, "the only one who realizes people get sick on weekends." We were fashioning hope from pitiful scraps. Dr. Graham was old and still kept Saturday hours; this meant fate had sent him to save us.

Mother and I stood on either side of Bonnie as she disrobed, staunch protectors not to be denied.

"It's the size of a nickel," said Doctor Graham, palpating

Bonnie's left breast. In his hands her flesh looked neutral, sexless. That night I would lie in my bed and try to imagine a flat nickel swollen into a sphere, its silver letters and numbers stretched and contorted. "We'll have it out," said the doctor in his own strange language of softened words and odd diction, meant to dispel fear. "And you're about twenty?"

"Nineteen," said Mother before Bonnie could answer.

He nodded. "Concern here is almost nonexistent." Beneath the examining light the skin on his cheeks looked varnished, faintly orange. "Breast cancer is very nearly an unheard of thing in young women." He smiled at Bonnie. "It's a disease of old ladies."

"Ninety percent harmless," Mother offered. It was a question.

"That's right!" the doctor replied, somehow giving too much enthusiasm to the words, as if speaking to children.

"And the scar will be very small," I announced, amazed at my own audacity. I was picturing a nickel lying against the soft expanse of Bonnie's ample breast, making a direct parallel between the coin's physical size and the scant worth of five cents.

We brought Bonnie home with us and Mother immediately called Dr. Horn at his residence. He confirmed the words of his colleague and even added additional encouragement. Bonnie's hormones were acting up; it was a common thing. The chances of a woman so young having breast cancer were infinitesimal.

"Hormones," said Father when we told him, letting his eyebrows rise and descend, testing his courteous smile for a moment and then retreating to a solemn expression that, in the end, revealed nothing. I am sure he meant his sober gaze to be his final judgment on the matter; he could not have guessed he would be consulted further.

There was a problem with Bonnie's medical insurance. She had neglected some step, signing a paper, perhaps filling out a form or paying a fee. The fault was clearly hers. The situation could be remedied, the insurance reinstated, but the process would require seven to ten days.

Now ensued a chain of events that in retrospect seem pathetic, even ludicrous. My mother decreed Bonnie should remain under Dr. Graham's care. This was partly superstitious hope that the good luck of his Saturday hours would carry us through to swift, easy victory. It was also part courtesy. Having gone to one doctor for treatment, it was awkward to leave him in the middle of things, a real rudeness in our community.

Dr. Graham required no forward payment of fees, but the hospital where the surgery would be done ruled that without insurance Bonnie would have to pay five hundred dollars in advance. I can picture a younger, more aggressive Dr. Horn talking the hospital down with a few swift words. I can see Bonnie taking out a bank loan, or phoning other relatives for the money. But the dozen ways we might have coped with the malignancy racing through her body have no validity. We put ourselves into the hands of Dr. Graham, and my father.

Mother's own purse could not be stretched beyond the loans of ten or twenty dollars. She had never earned a paycheck in her life. She asked Father for the money. I do not know what words passed between them, only their result.

Following the conversation, Father gathered all of us in the kitchen, looking little different but with some new energy flowing through him, lifting him up. "We will all sit down with the doctor," he announced, "and make a true determination of this situation." I think he intended to sound only deliberate, but his voice arched perilously and I saw that he was transformed, a man bent on humiliation, on object lessons as big as the sky. It was like magic gone wrong.

Within the hour, the four of us were facing Dr. Graham across his desk. Father appropriated all of this urgency to himself, stealing the drama from Bonnie, demonstrating with small, quick movements how much he had been inconvenienced. "If there is no real worry about cancer," he said to the doctor, "what is all the rush? Why can't we wait for the insurance to come through?" He was showing us his concern and logic were of a quality superior to ours, superior even to the doctor's. Feeling ourselves totally dependent, Mother, Bonnie, and I sat in silence, aching to have the money and be finished with Father.

In his years of practice had Dr. Graham seen countless different reactions to the threat of cancer, or only two or three repeated with endless variations? I can only know that on that day he misread my father, taking the strident words for the voice of fear. Clearly, he believed this man in his own pathetic way was trying to protect his family. The doctor's compassionate gaze never faltered.

Father got to his feet and began to move about the room. His voice now full of confidence, he discussed the value of money, the irresponsible attitudes of young people, the number of hours he had to work to earn five hundred dollars. I understood him perfectly. He did not think Bonnie worthy to have a serious illness; he believed her disease, rather, to be a fall from virtue.

In the end, there would be guilt enough for everyone. I could have helped my father. More than anyone, I knew of his fragile inner life, his terror of a garment factory that swallowed up young women only to disgorge them into mediocre marriages. I could have shown him a difference between Bonnie and me, a solid thing he could have trusted. Much as I loved my aunt, I already knew we were cut from different cloth. Instead, I stared out the window behind the doctor's head, watched the sun pass its zenith and begin to descend, while Father continued a performance that was all for me, meant to demonstrate beyond question that happiness was so elusive it might slip through the fingers as easily as an insurance form.

Dr. Graham finally broke in on this monologue. "Cancer,"

he said, "is not totally impossible. However, it is highly unlikely."

But Father had been carried out of himself. He was like someone newly rich, or a man naming all the things he was not afraid of. "My wife even got a second opinion!" he cried. "She asked Dr. Horn! Just to be sure! He said the same!"

Mother's head shot up in disbelief at this betrayal. She moved her lips as if to speak, then seemed to grasp that the thing done was now forever beyond retrieval. She began to blush, pink stains in her cheeks that widened, the color growing deeper, spreading into her neck. Then her head dropped, and she sat on in hot, wretched silence.

After this meeting, Father went to the hospital and paid the five hundred dollars as, I am sure, he had intended to from the beginning.

Bonnie's surgery was performed the following morning. The malignancy had spread to the lymph nodes in her armpit, and was already smoldering in her liver. A brief eight months later, she was dead.

Perhaps because she grieved so intensely, Mother was first to recover from Bonnie's death. She was more Steed than any of us had known, quicker to feel pain than the Porters, and also quicker to heal. After a time, speaking of Bonnie, she came to say only, "The problem with cancer is that it's hidden from sight." The words seemed to give her solace.

But Father fled from us into numb, gray silence. He continued to earn a living but he no longer worked about our house, grew a garden, nor advised me about my future. When I graduated from college, only Mother attended my commencement. She came elegantly dressed, her tinted hair neatly coiffed. As we lunched after the ceremony, she darted glances about the restaurant, like a single woman appraising men.

Bringing the News

*I*n July my husband Mark harvests the first plump green beans from the garden and thins out the tiny carrots. The carrots are not large enough to save but he saves them anyway. His large hands brush away the soil with small, scrupulous movements. Clad only in shorts and sandals, hunched above the garden foliage, his body looks powerful, tanned, and healthy. Only a few salty flecks of gray about the ears mark him as thirty-three and eight years married.

With his pocket knife, he carefully tops each tiny carrot and hands the lacy greens to Amy who stands beside him gathering them solemnly into a neat bouquet in the meticulous manner of a three-year-old who has been assigned an important task. The carrot tops will be a special treat for Bitsy, a plump brown rabbit who observes this Saturday morning idyl from the shelter of her cage, as I look on from the living room window. Watching, it occurs to me that Mark and Amy do not look like the family of a woman who has been raped. They look exactly like two people I knew a brief two months ago.

When the carrots have been topped, Mark rises a little stiffly, then brings his six-foot frame up to its full height, dwarfing Amy. He smiles and there is some exchange of banter I cannot hear. He picks up the pail of carrots and, with his free arm, lifts Amy. Safe in the bend of her father's arm, she rides serenely up into the air. Mark deposits her at the faucet beside the patio. He kneels, together they wash the small carrots. I grope for my customary Saturday contentment and find only a dull and empty sense of isolation.

Outside, Mark removes Bitsy from her cage. Clutched by her belly, the rabbit thrashes frantically, flailing the air with helpless legs. Her ordeal is over in one swift moment as Mark sets her free for a romp on the grass, a lunch of carrot tops, but I look away, sickened. I have commanded my mind not to play these tricks, but I seem ruled by some fretful stranger who wills what I should think and feel.

In the shadow of the patio, my husband's body moves like a cool, sleek machine. I discover that I am trying to understand him, as if he were a man I had just met.

I have no clear memory of Mark's presence in the hospital emergency room. I recall a clutter of voices, a shifting collage of faces. I remember, oddly, that my fingernails were caked with mud and that the palm of my left hand was streaked with blood. I believe it hurt Mark to learn that I did not remember more. I am sure he said courageous and comforting words to me, loving words. Later, a nurse told me he had pounded his fists against a wall, and then cried. I wish I could remember. Perhaps that memory would be the beginning of a bridge across the chasm that now separates me from my husband, an empty, silent space.

Amy and Mark return Bitsy to her cage and come into the kitchen for lunch with a grand sense of celebration. "Mama!" Amy summons me stridently. "We got theeese!" She tumbles the small, damp carrots onto the table and dances on her toes.

I mobilize some memory of myself and answer. "Marvelous!"

"They're delicious!" Mark's voice explodes in the small room. We are actors in Amy's drama. I search past noise and movement for the familiar fabric of our lives, and wonder if it ever existed.

Mark brings a warm washcloth and crouches on one knee beside Amy to wash her face. He pushes tousled hair care fully from her forehead. She twitches and he murmurs encouragement, tilting her chin upward to wash her tiny neck, "almost . . . just a touch more." The rising tone of his voice promises that the task is nearly done. Mark believes he is the only father who is raising a child in exactly the right manner. When he sees children in shops, in the park, or in the street, his eyes swiftly assess each one and catalog the parents' shortcomings. He has appointed himself an authority on neglected diapering, too-tight waistbands, dangerous toys, nutritious snacks. He struggles to remain silent and be charitable toward adults who take parenting lightly or who do not agree precisely with his views. He is convinced that no father has ever loved a child as intensely as he loves his daughter. I watch him and recall the gentle touch of my own father's hand.

Amy participates fully in this venture and accepts without question that she and Mark are unique human beings, set apart from all other daddies and little girls in an important and special way. She explores the latitude of her role and searches out her boundaries with curiosity and delight, testing the limits of both her power and her helplessness. To Mark's steadfastness she is, in turn, petulant, generous, coy, selfish, fearful, bold, courageous. In her father, a little girl seeks and finds all men.

At her plate, Amy toys now with her half-eaten sandwich, exhausted from the morning's excitement. She pulls the bread apart and nibbles at a piece of lettuce. I set things away and take her up for her nap. On the stairs, she hums a tuneless tune which, at the door of her room, becomes a fretful plea. "Sleep with me, Mama!" I welcome the chance to lie down. I am bone-tired with a weariness that sleep does not heal.

On the bed in her small, bright room Amy thrashes for a moment, clutches me, murmurs about her rabbit. She looks at the nursery figures on the wallpaper and yawns. In my own memory, I recall this process of going to sleep. These are the rituals we carry out to be certain we are safe.

When Amy is satisfied that all of the figures in her wall-paper are in precisely their proper places, and that the silky coverlet swishes against her bare legs with exactly the right sound, she closes her eyes and is instantly asleep. Her breathing is deep and regular. Tiny beads of perspiration appear on her forehead. In sleep, her small arm is raised and thrown against me.

When I was nine or ten, I belonged to the Camp Fire Girls. We met at seven in the evening in a basement room of our village library. One evening a girl named Lisa stayed after the meeting to discuss a project with Mrs. Hill, our leader. Later, as she was coming up the stairway alone, a man appeared from the shadows, clasped a hand over her mouth, and attempted to drag her away. Lisa managed to wriggle free and scream. Adults appeared. The man fled up the stairs and disappeared into the dark street.

This event became the subject of many furtive conversations among little girls, huddled in knots in backyards, clustered on the playground jungle gym, gathered behind closed bedroom doors. A chorus of fierce whispers: I would kick . . . oh I would kick . . . very hard . . . and bite too . . . bite too . . . anybody would . . . because I would never . . . nobody would . . . oh no . . . I'd scratch with my fingernails like this . . . I'd die . . . because you know . . . I know . . . everybody knows . . . because if you died you could go to heaven . . . I would definitely go to heaven.

When I was about to be raped, I discovered I did not wish to die. I wanted very much to live. The images that flashed through my mind at that moment were not really thoughts at all. I saw the afghan I had been crocheting. If I died, I knew my sister would complete it, and her stitch is tighter than mine. The result would be a sad, lopsided thing. Perhaps it would be given to Amy, a clumsy, botched object that would have to be cherished in my memory. And in time, my sister would teach Amy to crochet, in a fashion a little different from mine.

I recall quite clearly that my sister visited me in the hospital. The face of a nurse drifts into memory, efficient eyes looking down at me, a white world of soft, intermittent footsteps and the sharp odor of disinfectants. "Mrs. Warren . . . ? Sarah . . . ? Your sister is here."

My sister arrived like a hot wind, flushed cheeks, disheveled hair, breathless, agitated. For an instant she did not seem to know who I was. Then our hands locked in a familiar gesture and she pressed my fingers so tightly they turned a bluish gray and looked like useless dead things curled above the sheet. When she was able to speak, her voice was hoarse. "Sarah . . . you could have been killed." Trembling, she sat on the edge of the bed and pulled me to her. We held each other and cried, as we had cried so many times before, over a broken doll or a broken romance, as we cried when our mother died, as we cried when my sister's small son was stillborn. But these tears were different, I could feel distance between us. My sister's voice became a gentle, comforting hum. I listened to the words, and then past them, with growing disbelief. Her voice carried a note of rebuke. Although she did not say it she believed, and continues to believe, that in some way I am responsible for what has happened.

On that night, I did not alter my routine in any way, I performed no act to provoke another human being, I violated none of the rules for safe conduct. Yet, other women will believe I was somehow responsible for the attack upon me. I first learned this from my sister's voice.

Her words were really for herself. She believes if she carries out certain precautions she will never be raped. It is easier for her to think I failed in some way than to believe she is vulnerable.

I have forgiven her. Until now, I believed exactly as she does. Perhaps I still believe. If I had been able to think a powerful thought or say special words could I have prevented the attack? I still want to believe in Amy's kind of magic, that the things we do will always keep us safe. Mark tries very hard to understand all of these things. He listens intently to everything I say, as if I spoke a foreign language he must strain to understand. He assesses my words and keeps some invisible record where he charts the progress of my recovery.

There are two Marks now. A sane, clinical daytime man moves about with great control. In the morning, he ties his necktie with a neat little snap, as if to say, "See how well all of this is going?" As if he might be called upon at any time to demonstrate the tying of neckties. He finds great hope in trivial things. "Look here!" he cries. "See how the grass is coming back on the west side of the lawn." When he performs small tasks, he speaks of himself as *we*. "We'll be finished here in just a moment." Giving me assurance.

The second Mark is the tentative man who lies beside me each night. In the privacy of darkness, gazing out at the distant, impersonal stars, does he ask the same questions I ask? Do they twist and turn upon themselves? Why has this thing happened to me and not to another person? Does it serve some purpose I cannot discern? Will my phone ring some morning and a voice say, "We are so pleased with what you are doing, Sarah, for all our sakes"? I have held this experience in my hand and turned it every way, like a dark gemstone that catches the light with each facet and reflects at a hundred different angles, searching for resolution, and there is none. I do not know if it is possible to live and love in an unsafe world.

Now I separate myself from Amy, cover her lightly, close the door softly behind me. Mark has showered and stands in our bedroom in a pair of light trousers, barefoot, examining the pine paneling above the fireplace. Although my steps are almost soundless, he is aware of me. "The wood is lifting," he says. "Moisture is getting through. Perhaps we should have someone look at this chimney."

Beside him, I touch the warped wood. This bedroom is like a summary of our marriage. We built this room ourselves,

tearing out a partition and bringing two small rooms together, laying the fieldstone of the fireplace with our own
hands, building enormous closets, setting in casement windows, paneling the fireplace wall and papering the others
with a rich, textured wallpaper, laying the thick, soft ivory
carpet. This room has been our only luxury.

A wall of deep shelves holds the mementos of our life
together, our collection of Eskimo soapstone carvings, a Delft
pitcher Mark's mother brought us from Amsterdam, our wedding photograph, a bouquet of dried weeds contributed by
Amy, our two identical copies of Yeats from college years,
cherished from the day we discovered we both read the same
poetry.

Mark built our enormous bed and Amy was conceived
there. Beside the bed is the bentwood rocker we have dubbed
Great Heaven, because my sister said, "Great heaven, how
could you spend so much money on one chair?"

Mark's presence is sweet to me. His bare arms and shoulders smell faintly of soap and his damp hair gleams in the
light from the window. I touch his shoulder tentatively and
feel a small ripple of desire begin in my stomach and, with it,
fear, because the old pathways of easy, familiar feeling are
gone.

Mark's hand drops from the wall and he slips his arm
around my waist. There is silence, tense, loving, confused.
"What do you want?" he asks softly. And again, "Please tell me
what you want."

And now words from the dark side of my mind come
unbidden. I discover I am trembling. It is like the onset of
labor, coming in its own ripeness, a birthing that follows its
own necessities. "I'll tell you what I want," I say in a voice that
does not belong to me, fierce, petulant. "I want all of the
world to be angry *with* me, all of the people in the cities and
in the country, riding in buses and flying on airplanes. I want
some powerful act of retribution to occur . . . and that is not
going to happen. I want to be like Amy again, full of myself,

brimming with importance, happy, clean . . . instead of being broken . . . covered with a filth I can't wash off!" I am sobbing now. Mark grips my hand, as he did when Amy was born, and I descend into a strange room filled with brilliant light and gaudy color. It is my private hell of rage and shame, a place of mockery and degradation. My chest burns and it is difficult to breathe.

"It's all right, Sarah. It's all right now."

Mark is holding me. Then the sudden fit is past, my sobs subside, and my ears ring in the great hollow of silence about my head. "I am so very tired of crying."

"It's all right." Mark's voice is a small, cool wind against my damp cheek.

"I feel a little better now." Vision clearing, the deep swell of my own breathing, the fist of muscle in my chest melting. *Sensations.* Bringing me the news . . . of my own juices, patient and persistent. Regeneration that happens out of sight, the dark work of the cell. Somewhere an old sweater is coming out at last at the elbows. "I feel better now."

"I know."

"Mark, I'll always remember. It will still be there ten years from now, twenty . . . and even when we are old."

"But it's going to be all right. Believe me."

"I believe you."

Mark strokes my hair with a small, clumsy gesture that makes him seem very young, vulnerable. "Let's have a glass of lemonade!" he says suddenly, brightly, as if he had just invented lemonade. A sluggish memory stirs, and before he can speak again I know he will say, "Just let me get my shoes and grab a shirt."

I move to the window and stand in the swath of afternoon sun that falls on the soft carpet.

"Look," Mark says, coming up beside me, "see how the grass is coming back?"

I see that it is true. The grass is returning. Each day the pale, fragile tendrils grow stronger, greener.

"Lemonade," says Mark, gently taking my arm. "Amy will sleep for a little while."

And this is also true. Amy will sleep a little longer, in her child's body, in her child's bed. Then she will wake and thrust herself eagerly into the next hour, with its unknown joys, its unknown misfortunes. I take Mark's hand and say a short, silent prayer for my daughter, that she will always be shielded by hope, that she will always trust love's courage.

Amos

O ne day when Amos Haffner was eleven years old he knocked on the door of a house in a strange neighborhood and asked a woman for food. "I'm very hungry," he said. He had been hiking, trying out a new pedometer he had received in exchange for cereal boxtops. The pedometer was strapped to his ankle. It was full summer, a day filled with freedom and great hope. He had been pushing on toward ten miles, striding down street after street, half of Milwaukee it seemed, in a mad dream of clicking steps.

"Food?" The woman was huge and fierce-appearing with blazing red hair. Not until he saw her amazed face did Amos realize he had blundered. His request had been a bizarre act. He fled, shame overriding hunger. For a long time after, he feared his body might at any time act of its own volition, hurling him off a tall building, opening his trousers and exposing his private parts, causing him to vomit in church. His only consolation was that the woman did not know his name. Then he began to believe he had, indeed, spoken it. Following this, his shame seemed connected to the name itself, his peculiar, old-fashioned name. Outside his bedroom window in the small house he shared with his mother, grew a flowering plum that blossomed briefly in spring and was otherwise an ugly, dwarfish growth that was neither bush nor tree. As he sat in his room looking out of the window, the plum, which seemed to him caught and frozen forever between two states of being, became a correlative for the memory that tormented him. One day he took a rusting axe from a pile of tools in the back of the garage, moldering possessions left behind by his dead father, and cut down the flowering plum. But the memory of the woman did not go away for a long time.

Her image returned to him again thirty-one years later at the funeral of his wife Noreen. When he looked for the last time at Noreen's face, framed by the coffin's satin pillow, willing himself to experience the moment in some profound way, the amazed expression of the red-haired woman swam up from memory. At the little supper held in the church basement following the funeral, someone gave him a slice of pale green cake and he nibbled a few crumbs of it. It seemed the cake had been intended as mint, but the only flavor that had survived the baking was a bitter taste that made him think of chewing grass. Later, when he would recall Noreen's face in the coffin, the recollection was always accompanied by the memory of the cake's odd savor. Such things—the face of the woman, the taste of the cake—suggested to him that the world had a secret system of bookkeeping to shield its purposes from discovery. The system involved a code whose symbols were sense impressions. Sights. Sounds. Tastes. He dealt with his grief by telling himself events had purpose beyond human understanding.

The church was in Milwaukee, in the neighborhood where both he and Noreen had grown up. Its basement looked shabby and seemed little changed since his boyhood. He found the sight of it reassuring. The faded paint on the walls and the aging, scarred banquet tables told him his own life had momentum.

At the funeral supper family members, almost all of them Noreen's relatives, asked him questions.

"What will you do now?"

"Where will you live?"

"Do you think Noreen would want you to remain single?"

"Do you realize forty-two is so very young?"

"Can you appreciate she did not suffer?"

"Will you be afraid to drive a car now?"

"Will you need help?"

"What will you do?"

He answered all of them, "I don't know."

But when he returned alone to the apartment he had shared with his wife in Evanston, the answer to all of the questions came to him. "I will go on as before," he said aloud. His voice, touching the familiar furnishings like a caressing hand, sounded to him remarkably calm and capable.

The apartment was on the second floor of a large Victorian house. The first floor was rented to a cellist from the Chicago symphony. It was a commuter's neighborhood. Amos and Noreen had been among the hardier residents who walked to the train station daily for the trip into Chicago. The living room of the apartment featured a bow window that over-looked maple foliage in summer so that the room seemed to float free of the street. The windows were hung with heavy linen drapes, drawn in winter against the gray chill of the lake. In winter, Amos had laid fires in the elaborate old fire-place that still, miraculously, drew perfectly, and Noreen had served them meals on trays before the hearth.

She had been keen on antiques but scrupulous in her selections. There was a tall mahogany secretary and a fine gate-legged dining table, some Eastlake oak pieces, but the room was half empty. In spite of twelve years of marriage, five of them in this house, Noreen had not finished furnishing the living room. Still, Amos was accustomed to the space of the place and decided at once to leave things as they were. In addition to the living room, there were two bedrooms, a kitchen, and a bath. Because the rooms were unusually large, these few comprised the entire second floor of the house.

Amos made few changes in his routine. He gave up the breakfasts he and Noreen had shared daily in a coffee shop near the train station. He was uneasy sitting alone in restau-rants. He preferred now to eat at home, brewing a pot of coffee and sitting at the round table in his kitchen, looking down from a window into his neighbor's well-tended back-yard. He purchased small boxes of cereal and set them in a line on the kitchen counter, allotting one for each day and eating them in rotation so that no cereal ever became stale.

Noreen had always done the shopping. Amos shopped for groceries now on his way home from work. This change in his schedule caused him to arrive at his apartment a little later. He began to meet the cellist leaving as he came up the front steps of the house.

"Haffner!" The cellist was an intense man with thick eyebrows. Amos and Noreen had never made friends with their neighbors. The man's eyebrows repelled Amos; they suggested to him neglect and recklessness. "How are you, Haffner?"

"Fine. I'm fine, thank you."

He altered his schedule, lingering longer at the super-market, paging through magazines, to avoid meeting the cellist.

Amos was an engineer with an industrial firm in Chicago. The company made conveyors for warehouses and factories. At work, he sat on a high stool before a drawing board and drew layouts of components for conveyors. He also often served as the company's troubleshooter. He had a mechanic's eye, a mechanic's sensitive fingers. When machinery broke down, he was sent for to discover the cause. His company had stayed on in old buildings within the city when others had moved out to suburban industrial parks to rebuild and retool. The conveyor company was now flanked by empty factories. Sometimes when Amos sat at his drawing board, he sensed the emptiness beyond the walls, as if the world were receding. One day he might walk out of the door and find nothing but silent space where the city had been. It reminded him of a scene in a movie he and Noreen had seen; after a nuclear holocaust, a single leaf, borne by a wisp of wind, danced through empty, silent streets.

When machines failed, Amos sometimes traveled to the site to make an inspection, occasionally flying to a distant city, but most malfunctioning equipment was brought into the plant's shop for work, into a large high-bayed area where small components had once been built on an assembly line. This work was now farmed out overseas. When Amos worked here he was usually the only person in the large, gloomy space. His tools echoed against the concrete floor. But the windows of the room were oddly placed. When he stood in an outside doorway, his body blocked out nearly all daylight from the room.

Amos prided himself on being immaculately clean. After working on machinery, he cleaned his hands carefully, in a three-stage process. He never left the area with grease under his nails nor embedded in the cuticle of his fingers.

The secretary for the engineering department was a young woman with straight black hair. She wore contact lenses that caused her much difficulty. She had always to be taking them out and putting them back in. One day when Noreen had been dead for a month, the secretary came out to the shop where Amos was working and began telling him about reincarnation. "Edgar Cayce says we lived lives before this one and will live again." Amos sensed she was a spokesman for all of the people in his office. He wondered if the others knew the direction her conversation would take. "The seeds of a flower fall into the earth and grow again. Everything is a cycle. It's an accepted idea in Eastern religions."

Amos was kneeling beside a gear box, holding a socket wrench. He pictured the girl reading the little paperbacks on Eastern religions, struggling to see through the troublesome contact lenses. The only Eastern religion he could immediately think of was Buddhism.

"The men want you to play cards with them on the lunch hour." She said the words as if asking a favor.

Most often, he spent his lunch hour reading technical magazines. He had no objection to playing cards. "All right." He began playing euchre with the men, a game he had played with his mother as a child. He discovered he could predict how a hand of cards would fall with almost perfect accuracy after the first trick, at most the second, had been played.

It was four months after the funeral when he realized his behavior had become compulsive. He asked the produce manager of the supermarket to open a sealed bag of oranges and sell him exactly seven, one for each day of the week. The revelation amused him. Seeing himself in the manager's eyes as an eccentric gave Amos satisfaction. It suggested that in these four months, without his being aware of it, he had constructed some identity of his own, separate from Noreen. He walked off with his oranges a bit jauntily and imagined himself telling someone, I am a man to be reckoned with. This sentence struck him as very clever. When he was alone outside on the street, he laughed out loud, as if demonstrating his competence to an invisible listener.

And the sound of his own voice led him into a softly murmured monologue: My wife and I liked routine. People may have found us unimaginative but I prefer to think we were just well adjusted to our circumstances. We did not ponder life at great length. That served us well as a couple, but it has left me ill-equipped to deal with disruption. I have been unable to project myself into either abject grief or any new, purged plane of existence for the future.

The sight of his own house looming up from the evening shadows startled him. He attempted to laugh as he had before and could not. Perhaps I am a little mad, he thought.

On Sundays, Amos took his car from the garage and drove to church. After church, he often drove to his mother's small house in Milwaukee. This represented little change in his routine. He and Noreen had almost always gone to church, and had made frequent Sunday trips to Milwaukee to visit Amos's mother, his only relative, or Noreen's assortment of relations.

Because they had not had children, Amos and Noreen had

maintained their status as a young couple in Noreen's large family far longer than was customary. Noreen, who had begun as a clerk at Marshall Field's and advanced to the position of buyer, had remained to her family a young career sister, trim and well dressed. It was assumed she had no time to cook and she was relieved of the task of carrying in cakes and casseroles for family dinners. She and Amos came empty-handed and ate heartily. In return, Noreen remembered the birthday of each brother and sister, niece and nephew, with a tasteful gift from Marshall Field's. Amos was seen (Noreen's sisters told her everything, and she told Amos) as clever and worldly. The other men envied him his freedom from family responsibility. They believed he was involved in activities he did not mention. The brothers and brothers-in-law consulted him about car repairs, mortgage interest rates, camping trailers.

"I don't know any more about this than you do," he tried to reply.

They did not believe him. "Amos, does it sound like the carburetor?"

"I suppose so." He was helpless against them. His in-laws took his modest manner as respect for them. They believed he was deeply concerned for their welfare. In a crisis, Amos would stand by the family. Amos and Noreen had money. They were saving and would soon be doing something fine, buying an expensive house, perhaps they would still have children.

In fact, Amos's simple life was merely an extension of the life he had shared with his mother. For Noreen, their quiet existence had been an escape from the turbulence of a large family. For both of them, frugality was a hedge against need; both had been raised in precarious financial circumstances. As a couple, they had not indulged themselves beyond the necessities of good clothing to wear to work, most of which Noreen purchased with her employee's discount. Otherwise, their only extravagances had been breakfast out, an occasional supper at a good restaurant, and fresh fruit for their table all year. They did not attend the theater; they rarely entertained; they still used the cast-off floorlamps Amos's mother had given them years before. Noreen sometimes purchased an antique, they saved their money. Their savings were not nearly as great as Noreen's relatives imagined them to be.

Shortly after the funeral, Amos stopped visiting Noreen's family. He had never felt a need to be close to anyone other than his wife. Now when he drove to Milwaukee, he saw only his mother.

In August, Amos observed his forty-third birthday. On the Sunday following, he made a special point of going to Milwaukee, knowing his mother would prepare a special meal and a cake for the two of them. She was a tiny, erect woman with an alert blue-eyed expression he recognized as much like his own. She had been a hairdresser and, at seventy, still took pains to arrange her own graying hair carefully. She wore silky floral-print dresses, all of which looked alike to Amos, and teetered about in shoes with Cuban heels and satin laces.

Her name was Leona and Amos had always associated the sound of it with great sadness. It seemed to him this had begun at his father's funeral when a shifting crowd of relatives, distant cousins he now supposed, had appeared briefly and then disappeared forever. He had been seven. The strangers spoke her name over and over. Leona . . . Leona. He had always heard his mother called Mrs. Haffner. Once he had tried to recall the sound of his father's voice speaking his mother's name, and had not been able to do so.

She was a quiet, industrious woman. If she was not especially cheerful, neither did she make an issue of the hardships she had encountered, in the way of other widows Amos knew. Yet he had always seen her as the survivor of a dreadful calamity. To Noreen he had once said, "It seemed a shameful thing that I was so small and powerless, that she had to look after me instead of my caring for her." In the years following his father's death, he had had many fantasies in which he apologized elaborately to his father and struggled to set the roles of mother, father, and child into some reasonable context. That his mother was self-sufficient and uncomplaining had not eased his suffering. As a child, he had at times tried to provoke her in the hope that she would accuse him openly of his shortcomings and say certain things that had never been said, dark things he could not accurately define.

Despite this exaggerated concern for his mother, he had never felt especially close to her. It seemed to him she surrounded herself with a fragile shell of daily routine that broached no intrusion. As a boy he had believed, in fact, that to come close to her might in some dreadful way destroy them both. Their existence depended upon her ability to rise each morning and pursue the day's challenges, one after another, keeping taut the invisible thread of their existence. He was convinced she suffered unspoken torments, as he did. Sometimes it had seemed to him he possessed some awful destructive power, and that if he went to his mother and laid his hand softly upon hers, all of the structure of their lives might collapse into unbearable grief, leaving them helpless. He had eventually dealt with these anxieties by forming a role he could play. A set of instructions. It was his task to maintain exactly the proper distance between them and thus obtain a perfect balance, much in the way a planet and its satellite move together and yet separately. The pattern had served him now for many years.

On the Sunday following his birthday, his mother finished eating her cake and poured cream from a pitcher into a small bowl. "Mrs. Kretchmer died last week," she said. "You remember Mrs. Kretchmer, don't you?"

"Of course."

"She had leukemia, the slow kind. There are two kinds, fast and slow." His mother kept a yellow cat which she called

Tommy. She set the bowl of cream on the floor beside her chair. The cat roused himself from his corner and came forward sluggishly to lap from the bowl. "She had always been Catholic," his mother continued, "but rather in the European fashion, not too devout. You know."

"Yes."

"But at the last she had the priest come every day and give her communion."

Amos continued to sip his coffee. He took no interest in his mother's accounts of the dead and the dying, and no response was required of him. Noreen's death had been very different. He did not associate it in any way with the deaths of others, especially the systematic business of simply growing old and dying. He suspected his mother would die soon.

"One of her sons wanted to have her cremated but the daughters wouldn't hear of it. Olive, the youngest, cried and stormed about it."

Amos rose, refilled their coffee cups, and returned to the table. The kitchen was clean and orderly but he saw that the linoleum was wearing through.

"They buried her but Olive couldn't be consoled, knowing her brother would even consider such a thing. You remember Olive Kretchmer. She's Olive Godowski now."

"She was ahead of me in school."

"Yes, Olive must be nearly fifty now."

"Mother, would you like a new linoleum? You can pick it out and charge it to me. I'll put it down the next time I come."

She did not want the linoleum and after dinner he drove back to Evanston, leaving early to be ahead of the traffic. He was home before six and spent an hour reading the paper. Then he carried his month's bills from the secretary to the round table where the light was better and sat down to write checks. A light wind sprang up outside, brushing maple branches against the house. The sound troubled him and he rose to draw the drapes. As he did so, he saw the dappled light of the streetlamps filtering through the branches and dancing on the carpet. The pattern of light and shadow came to rest as the wind died, began again as it rose. It was as if some restless presence had entered the room. Watching the shapes scatter and then reform, he found himself filled with anticipation. He thought perhaps it would rain soon and found this a pleasant prospect. But when he had drawn the drapes and returned to his seat at the table, anticipation became apprehension. It seemed to him he had left some task undone. He rose and checked all of the windows in the apartment to assure himself they were closed. He checked the gas burners in the kitchen, bending his head until he saw the stove's pilot light safely flickering.

He returned to the table, annoyed that he had permitted this interruption and, in a firm hand, wrote a check to the electric company. But when it had been written, he saw that he had entered the date of the previous year. His sense of apprehension grew. It seemed incredible that he could have made such an error. As an engineer, he wrote and drew each day and had a record that was unmatched for error-free work. The apprehension became a tightness across his chest. Then he considered that he had caught the error almost instantly, and before the check had been slipped into an envelope. But this thought, rather than giving him assurance, filled him with panic. He could not comprehend how his reason could depart so swiftly and then return capriciously.

He drew himself erect in his chair and with firm, deliberate movements wrote a second check that was correct in every way. This act brought relief. Then the cause of his unease seemed clear to him. His chest relaxed and he drew in a great breath of air. He needed to write, not merely to write but to record certain things in a small, black journal. He could see this book perfectly in his imagination. It seemed a thing he had known about for months, known and not known, a thought hovering just outside consciousness. Excitement swept over him. He discovered he was trembling.

It was still early evening. Taking his raincoat, he left the apartment and walked to a drugstore. He went directly to the stationery shelf and began to search for the book he saw so clearly in his mind. It was not there. He found an appointment register and a record book for double-entry bookkeeping.

He left the store and began to walk. A light rain fell and the wind grew sharp but he felt no chill. The exhilaration that had sprung up in him as he sat at the table still sustained him. He could feel that his face was hot and pink. His hands and feet seemed slightly swollen, as if his body held more blood than usual.

At a cross street, some impulse caused him to shift his gaze and he found himself looking directly into the lighted window of a small grocery store only a few doors away. He had never seen it before, although he was still less than a mile from his apartment. It was as if the store had appeared by magic, out of nowhere. Hatless and now quite wet, he walked quickly to the door and entered. An old woman with her hair wrapped in a knotted scarf looked out at him over a large jar of pickles. It seemed to Amos she was really a gypsy and he had interrupted her just as she was about to cast a spell over the pickles. "I need a notebook," he said abruptly. "Do you have stationery?" Then he saw it, a small, black book labeled *Journal* in gold letters, lying beside a box of school tablets. He felt as if he had arrived barely in time, that even a few minutes later the book would have been gone. He paid the woman and thrust the book inside his raincoat. Then he plunged back into the rainy night.

By the time he reached his own house, he had become calm. He felt as if he had performed a heroic act under desperate circumstances. As he came up the steps, it occurred to him that no one had seen him set out, and there was no one now to observe his return. The thought gave him satisfaction.

He hung his raincoat carefully over the bathtub and felt the security of familiar walls holding him. He laid the black book on the round table and the sight of it gave him pleasure. It looked exactly like an appointment book or daily calendar, except that the lined pages inside were completely blank. It seemed to him this design was very clever. The simple inscription *Journal* betrayed nothing, but inside the modest black cover, the pages could hold anything, absolutely anything.

He felt no rush now. He moved through the rooms arranging objects, turning down his bed, changing into his pajamas. From time to time he glanced at the book and felt joy in its lying so casually on the table. Finally, he made a sandwich and ate it. Then, opening the journal, he wrote his wife's name on the first page: Noreen Elizabeth Haffner, née Schwartz. Then he put the book in a drawer of the secretary, went to bed, and fell asleep almost immediately.

At work the next morning, Amos's supervisor assigned him a new job. He was to design a mounting frame for a conveyor that would carry crates at a fish processing plant. He said to his supervisor, "Once in a marsh I saw a squirrel with a small fish in its mouth."

"I didn't know they ate fish," the man replied.

"They don't. There was no explanation for it."

"Was the fish dead?"

"Oh yes," said Amos.

Carrying the layouts back to his table, Amos felt his mind was remarkably clear. It seemed to him he had never grasped a new job so quickly. He spread a clean sheet of vellum on his drawing table and found that he saw the lines on it even before he drew them.

At lunchtime, on impulse, he told his supervisor, "I have an urgent errand." He took a cab to the aquarium. When he arrived, he bought a fat pretzel from a street vendor and found it was quite enough to satisfy his hunger. He and Noreen had visited the aquarium a long time ago. He recalled she had been fascinated by the trout that hung motionless for long periods of time so that they seemed nearly to disappear and then, without discernible motive, darted swiftly to the other end of the tank, only to take up again their poised waiting.

She had said, "It's as if something dreadful is happening in there, something we can't see."

He went directly to the trout tank. It did not surprise him that he found his way easily, even though he had not been in the building for several years. Watching the trout whose habits had not altered—could they even be the same fish?—it occurred to him that he had always had an excellent memory. This thought filled him with happiness; it was like discovering a forgotten bank account that contained a sizable sum of money. His memory was a talent he had never fully utilized, that might still be developed into a valuable asset. He suddenly laughed out loud. A child standing nearby looked up and smiled.

On the taxi ride back to his office, he set himself the task of naming in advance each street he would cross and accurately spelling out its name. His score was perfect and he returned to his afternoon's work with such enthusiasm that the men around him seem buoyed by it. It was as if a small, pleasant event had occurred in the room.

That evening, he took the black journal from its drawer and, under Noreen's name, wrote a single word: Trout. It was clear to him now that the journal was not intended to hold a long and detailed account of any sort but rather, simply, a list of words. At the middle of the week, he wrote a postcard to his mother: "I will not be coming on Sunday. I will call you."

In church the following Sunday, he found himself too distracted to concentrate on the service. He had purchased a detailed map of the Chicago area. It made a comfortable bulge in the inner pocket of his coat. As the choir sang its anthem and the offering was taken, he longed to spread out the map and pore over it. Actually, he found that he did not need it. He seemed to remember every detail of the city—indeed of his life—with complete accuracy, especially the places he had visited with Noreen. On each day since he had bought the journal, a new set of memories had flooded his mind. An event that seemed initially vague would suddenly be embellished with a richness of particulars. All of these things seemed to organize themselves without his knowledge and then come spilling into consciousness. At the end of the service, he moved through the crowd quickly and found his car. His destination was an amusement park with a roller coaster and a funhouse. He and Noreen had visited the place shortly before their marriage. At the park, he bought a bag of popcorn and walked along the midway. He had forgotten to eat lunch and the popcorn tasted delicious. After an hour, he drove home. That night he wrote in his journal: Roller Coaster. Then he called his mother in Milwaukee. She told him his former high school history teacher had suffered a stroke and was not expected to live. She did not ask him how he had spent his day. As his mother talked, he spread his map on the table and studied it.

On succeeding Sundays, he visited a restaurant in Long Grove, the Museum of Science and Industry, the Lincoln statue in the Chicago Public Library. He drove to Indiana and walked along the beach, feeling the coming winter in the lake breeze. He visited a factory where glassware and china were made and sold—he and Noreen had purchased dinnerware there—and then could think of nothing to buy. At last, he chose a set of five small ceramic kittens and carried them off in a white gift box to a nearby restaurant. While he waited for his meal, he took the kittens from their tissue paper and set them in a line on the table. They were a dull peach shade, which to Amos suggested human skin. They crouched and leapt in playful poses, big-eyed and cherubic, their features expanded to suggest human faces. Then Amos understood why he had chosen them. These were the faces of his dead children, frozen in the poses of their last moments of life, children who had never been born and yet lived out some existence in a dimension beyond comprehension. These ideas did not sadden him; nothing saddened him these days. Rather, they seemed to stretch his perception; he could feel it as a physical thing, a prickling sensation at his temples, as if dormant tissue were coming back to life.

A young waitress brought his plate. "How sweet!" she said, indicating the kittens.

Amos smiled. "Yes, they're nice, aren't they?"

At home that night, he set the kittens on a shelf above the couch and recorded their existence in his journal. Then he named them and wrote the names in the book: Jonathan, Robert, Esther, Lucille, Franklin. He wrote quickly, as if these names were very familiar to him.

At his office, Amos began to talk to the men around him. He still worked quickly and efficiently—his supervisor had praised him and recommended him for a raise in pay—but he now discovered that he could carry on a conversation as he worked, a feat that had seemed impossible to him before. "I drove out to Wheaton on the weekend," he might begin. Then he would produce an accurate recital of everything that had occurred on his trip, the features of the landscape, the location of shops and restaurants, the activities of people he had seen, their clothing, their laughter and earnest words. Even the weather. "There was a light fog in the morning. It lay in the trees like smoke. It was an hour before the sun broke through and a fresh breeze sprang up."

The men around him followed the accounts with interest, urging him to continue when he paused. They told him it was wonderful he could discover so many interesting things in ordinary places and recall them in such detail. Finally they told him, one by one and in quiet tones, how pleased they were he was coming out of his grief.

Amos knew now that he was a little mad. He felt no concern about it. He could not in any case have altered the processes that had taken over his life. They were more powerful than his will, and they brought him pleasure.

He worked beside a tall, burly Italian named Vito Ricordi, a good-natured man who did tolerable work as a draftsman and played cards with grave passion. One afternoon Vito said to Amos, "How about taking a drive with me Saturday morning? I want to look at a car that's for sale somewhere out past

Downers Grove. I have the address but I don't know my way around out there, and you're sure a guy that never gets lost!" Vito laughed and looked around him, as if to assure himself his humor had been received and appreciated. "If I decided to buy it, you could drive my car back."

Amos suspected—indeed, with his new sensibility, was quite certain—that Vito simply wished to associate himself with Amos. He thought with amusement: My stories have made me a celebrity; now I will have hangers-on.

When Vito read off the address of the car's owner, Amos recognized the area at once. "I'll go with you," he said. "I like the drive out there."

For the rest of the week, Vito hung over Amos in a familiar way, patting his shoulder and taking great interest in the drawing Amos was making. He talked of the car he hoped to buy, a classic Lincoln Continental made in 1941. He offered information about himself, that he still lived with his parents, that his father was a butcher famous for his sausage in the Italian community. He discussed plans for the day endlessly, reminding Amos again and again that he would pick him up promptly at nine o'clock, that Amos should watch out of his window for a green Chevrolet.

Vito omitted only one detail. When Amos came down from his apartment on Saturday morning in answer to the insistent honking of the Chevrolet's horn, he found a large gray cat sitting on Vito's left shoulder. The cat was leaning out of the window sniffing the air solemnly. "This is Christopher!" Vito announced, grinning widely. "You know, like St. Christopher, patron saint of travelers?" Vito laughed. "You get it?"

Amos smiled and nodded. He found Vito, despite his fawning, pleasant company. The big Italian reminded him a little of Noreen's brothers and he felt a twinge of nostalgia for the relatives he no longer visited. He got into the car beside Vito and Christopher immediately hopped onto the back of the seat to sniff Amos's ear. Amos looked at the cat and would have attempted to stroke him but Christopher, his curiosity satisfied, suddenly sprang away. One graceful leap carried him to a small shelf under the car's rear window. He arranged his body in the narrow space and was instantly asleep.

"I have to get gas yet," said Vito, apologizing. "I would have already but nothing opens until nine." They drove to a nearby station and Vito filled his tank. A sleepy attendant had to locate a key and unlock a money box to find change. He carried the bills and coins to the car and thrust them through the window at Vito. At this motion, Christopher came awake. In one swift leap, he was on Vito's shoulder, crouched murderously in the car window, mouth open, a gutteral screech roiling up from his throat. Amos was astonished. It was the most repellent sound he had ever heard.

The attendant jumped back in fear and anger but Vito broke into laughter. "Christopher thought you were going to touch me!"

The man was not amused. "Mister, you get that damned beast out of here!"

Vito laughed harder. "As long as no one touches me, nothing happens!"

At a signal from Vito, a small flick of his hand, Christopher closed his mouth as quickly as he had opened it, but he maintained his perch on his master's shoulder, a sullen, wary sentinel.

As they drove off, Amos watched the cat in fascination. He had never feared animals. As a boy, he had often made excursions into the marshes near Lake Michigan, capturing small snakes, searching for turtles, or simply standing in shoulder-high marsh grass listening for birds. Once the circulation manager of the newspaper had paid him double wages to take a paper route where an unusual number of dogs menaced carriers. Four other boys had quit the route because of the dogs, but Amos had no fear of them and the dogs seemed to realize it. He had the route for more than two years and collected something of a small fortune in pay and tips. Christopher, the sentinel cat, amused Amos.

It was quickly apparent that Vito knew his way quite well; he had simply been seeking Amos's company. Amos did not mind. He liked Vito more and more. The man's loud good nature complemented his own quiet ways. It seemed to Amos that the two of them were in league, on some mysterious, hazardous errand. Christopher, stretched out and sleeping now beneath the rear window, heightened Amos's satisfaction.

It was November. They drove past tall, elderly houses that seemed defeated by time and the constant, wearing jar of the city; past men and women coming out to test the air as if to assure themselves the life of autumn was indeed gone. To Amos, Vito's Chevrolet was a capsule of warmth and vigor that would yet defeat some lurking adversary: the deadly routine of the days, winter perhaps, and even death itself. On street corners, people were buying newspapers. Amos fantasized that they might all turn to the same page at the same time and discover a marvelous news item, some joyous outrageous thing, and that the whole city might suddenly smile, so that the tired houses and littered streets would recede like an enemy routed, and color would flow back into the gray November faces of the people.

And yet he did not hate the city. He had come to love it, in fact, above nearly all things, perhaps as much as he loved his mother. This idea, tumbling suddenly into his mind, took him by surprise. The idea grew to enormous size, filling all of the space around him. Then it dwindled to nothing, a thing that had swept by before he could comprehend it. He understood that in some way Vito had replaced his mother. He could find no order in this curious progression of thoughts.

Vito had not stopped talking about the car he hoped to buy. "People ask why would you put your money into something that any way you look at it is going to be an old car." In his intensity, he became tangled in the language. Amos wondered if he had spoken Italian before he spoke English. "So you say classic car and what does it mean to people? Either you go for it or you don't."

For the first time in months, Amos thought of his own tangled car, of his wife lying dead within it. It was a picture that seemed to move toward him as if coming into focus, and then recede.

Vito had abandoned all pretense of not knowing his way. He had, in fact, turned off the main road for a leisurely drive through city streets, as if deliberately delaying the time when he would view the car. Amos supposed he needed more time to talk about it, or was perhaps apprehensive, that having planned so long for this day, he feared disappointment.

"Have you owned classic cars before?" Amos asked.

"I had a Model A once but it wasn't much, not like this. It wasn't anything special. You know what I mean? Special?" He turned to look directly into Amos's face, and Amos saw how great his friend's anxiety really was.

"I believe I do, Vito."

"Yeah, you do! You're the kind of guy that understands a special thing like that!" His angst was greater than anything he could express in words and he drove on silently for a time, gripping the steering wheel. Amos did not know how to help him.

The Lincoln Continental surpassed all of Vito's expectations. It filled Amos with wonder as well. A deep regal blue, perfectly restored, it sat in a driveway like a huge blue-black panther, sleek, well fed, alert, ready to spring. Vito circled it again and again. The love in his throat was so great he could scarcely speak for a time. To Amos, the car seemed an anomaly, an object plucked from another world and set down incongruously in this driveway in Downers Grove. It recalled to him a picture he had seen of an Oriental holy man in flowing robes walking among American army troops. The holy man had looked out on the disheveled soldiers with complete serenity, as if they and not he were out of place. The intensity of this thought startled Amos and brought him up short. He realized Vito's exuberance had drawn him in. He was tempted to see their circuitous drive to this place as a journey into a labyrinth that had at its center—he thought for a moment of the irony—an automobile. He turned his eyes away from the car and stared resolutely at the strip of sidewalk beneath his feet, reaching out for it with his mind. When he raised his eyes, he could see Vito through the window of the owner's house, sitting at a table filling out the papers that would transfer ownership of the Continental. Amos watched for a moment and the sight of this ordinary task, the act of writing on paper with a pen, restored his equilibrium.

"Hey Amos!" Vito called, coming down the steps of the house. Vito was suddenly composed, nearly cold with concern. "I'll go first so I can see how it handles and you follow. The guy said it had gas but you never know, right?"

Amos nodded and took the keys Vito handed him. He glanced at the Lincoln and saw that it was, after all, only a large, old-fashioned car. "I'll be right behind you." Then it seemed to Amos that the moment required something more, some gesture of comradeship. As he reached to open the door of the Chevrolet, his other hand went forward to touch Vito's shoulder.

Christopher's attack was swift and soundless. From somewhere in the depths of the Chevrolet, he sprang. Amos saw the mass of gray fur alight on his arm an instant before he felt the cold teeth sink into his hand and the needle-sharp claws lock into the flesh of his forearm.

"My god! Oh my god!" Vito cried. He pulled the cat away so quickly that the curled claws tore the flesh on Amos's arm in small diagonal grooves. The grooves were white for an instant before they filled with oozing blood.

The pain was brief and Amos felt oddly calm. He blamed himself entirely, for he had known Christopher's habits well in advance. It was as if the cat, like a clever chess partner, had waited until Amos was distracted to make his move. "It's nothing, Vito," he said. "Nothing at all." He found a tissue and wiped his arm; the bleeding stopped immediately. The meat of his hand, between thumb and forefinger, where the cat had embedded its teeth, did not pain him in the slightest.

The drive to Vito's home was accomplished without incident. In celebration, Amos agreed to eat Saturday supper with Vito's family. Included were four large, noisy brothers. The brothers were now completely repentant, filled with enthusiasm for the Continental. They laughed gross laughter and inspected the car as if it were a long-awaited newborn child that brought great honor to the family. Vito's mother served a hearty meal and touched her moist eyes from time to time with a handkerchief as if, it seemed to Amos, having produced this dining room full of male strength was a miracle beyond belief. Vito's father gave Amos a cigar and reminisced about 1941, the year the car had been built. When Vito took out his keys to drive Amos home in the green Chevrolet, Amos rose reluctantly.

That night he wrote in his journal: Vito, Lincoln Continental. And after it, for the first time, he wrote a sentence on the page. "Love and happiness blur into one and sit above pain patiently, waiting to strike." He did not know what the curious words meant. He wrote the sentence a second time, as if taking dictation from another person. This time his hand trembled and he felt beads of perspiration on his forehead. He recalled the curious thoughts about his mother that had come to him on the drive to Downers Grove, and the strange sensations he'd felt looking at the Lincoln. The buoyancy he had known for weeks drained away. He felt tricked. It seemed to him that all of the events since Noreen's death had led him in an insidious way to this moment. A plan beyond comprehension had been at work arranging his destruction. He felt now the full onslaught of a powerful enemy.

Weakness overtook him. He glanced about the apartment

but could not rouse himself to the simple task of hanging up his coat. Panic began and then subsided. There was no strength in him to sustain it. He looked at the open journal and saw that it was a condemnation of him. Madmen kept such journals, wrote incomprehensible words in small, secretive books. Its discovery would injure him; he would be taken off to a madhouse. Through his daze, he could clearly sense a place with crisp white bedsheets and locked doors, a place of despair. He wondered briefly if Vito would come to visit him. Along with the memory of Vito came a warm feeling of family, not only Vito's but Noreen's, a sharp sense of his mother, and of Noreen herself. These entered his mind and then retreated, sucked into a black vortex of dizziness and confusion. He felt cold sweat at the back of his neck.

Yet a portion of his mind continued to operate with clarity. He was like a man drowning who suddenly grasps a piece of slippery wood and wills his fingers to move carefully along it until it can be held firmly, obligatory, primal motions to prevent its slipping away. He understood that he had to destroy his journal. Without it in his possession, he would receive more humane treatment. The ordinary objects in his apartment would not betray him. He could hear a voice saying, I don't think it's really much at all. Nothing unusual was found among his possessions.

With great effort, he tore the used pages from the book, ripped them into shreds, and carried them to the toilet. Weak and trembling, he stood above the whirling water and flushed the toilet four times. Then he raised the seat and studied the bowl carefully to be sure that every shred of the incriminating paper had disappeared. He carried the rest of the book, now bearing no mark of ownership, into the outer hallway and, when he had assured himself that no one else was present, dropped it into a communal wastebasket. Then he returned to his apartment and fell into bed.

He awoke once during the night to find a stripe of moonlight shining across his bed and directly into his face. The moonlight was cold as snow. He shifted under his blanket and discovered that he was shivering, soaked with perspiration. He recalled the fragments of notepaper swimming in the turgid water of the toilet bowl; he thought of the swiftly darting trout at the aquarium moving to safety a hair's breadth ahead of some silent, unseen predator. He felt reassured. He understood that he had put his life into other hands. Childlike, he waited for dim figures to appear and take charge of him. As he fell into stuporous sleep, the aching of his body seemed not pain at all, but a serene pressure formed by the moonlight pressing his body down against the bed.

For the first days of his illness, his periods of lucidity were too brief to form events in his mind. Later, he would remember he had called a nurse to his bed in the middle of the night to tell her everyone in the hospital was dying. He saw death like frigid moonlight stirred into an icy froth of fog edging down each hallway of the building, floor by floor, freezing all life in its path into grotesque ice forms.

When he was stronger, his consciousness moved from this barren floor of his mind with its giant phantasmagorias to a higher plane. His hallucinations became hard-edged and dramatic. Then he believed that all of the functions of his mind were operating with clarity but that their ultimate control had been given over to some canny stranger.

He knew the facts of his illness as if they were a given, the information transmitted to him through some osmotic process. He was suffering from tetanus, a bacillus carried on the teeth and claws of the malevolent Christopher. His doctors had been amazed at the swift onset of the disease, and so inexperienced in treating it they had had difficulty with the diagnosis. Had one of them said, Here is a specter from the Middle Ages? Or had he imagined that? Vito, sick with remorse, had turned Christopher over to be examined for rabies—which he did not have—and then ordered the cat destroyed.

Amos knew the severity of his illness and his dogged cling-
ing to life had stirred interest in the medical community, and
that the men and women who moved in and out of his room
represented some of the finest medical minds in the Middle
West. He knew he was not in a madhouse and remembered,
thankfully, how well his mind had operated just before his
collapse. He assured himself again and again that the notebook was gone forever. He considered himself a madman
masquerading behind legitimate illness.

He could not recall how he had been discovered and trans-
ported to the hospital. It was a small concern that would
eventually be explained to him. Nor did he remember the
arrival of his mother who now sat at the foot of his bed, a
more or less permanent feature of his room. He knew he was
sedated to prevent injury and that the medication contributed to his confusion.

He fretted about his mother for it seemed to him she still
worked in the beauty shop, that these idle days would bring
financial ruin to both of them. He saw her young again, standing in the shop hour after hour until her ankles puffed
with edema, or sitting at the kitchen table calculating their
monthly bills against her earnings.

Memories merged so that it seemed to him it was his
mother's cat that had attacked him, as he attempted to
deliver a newspaper to his own home. He could feel the sharp
teeth plunging into his hand with such force that he was sent
reeling from his bicycle. He felt the dull shudder as his body
slapped against the gravel of the driveway, and even heard
the eerie ping of a bicycle pedal spinning as the wheel came
down against his face, pinning him against sharp stones.
Many distressing memories of this early world tormented
him. It was a world of broken bicycles, damaged clothing,
clumsiness, failure of every sort.

He discovered that a host of images had long lain dormant
in his brain, a gaudy zoo of creatures that drifted in and out of
consciousness. One day it seemed he was struggling to open

121

the door of a phone booth in a frenzy to make an important call. The phone booth was of a fashion he had not seen in many years. When the door at last yielded, he discovered a small, thin man of incredible age with deeply lined, almost mummified skin smiling at him with amber eyes. He knew it was his father, an ancient wisp of memory pressed grotesquely between the folds of his mind, a powerful polarity operating at once to preserve and destroy him.

The metaphor of a zoo returned again and again. Animal-like creatures moved at will through iron bars, through walls, like persistent drafts of air on a windy day. There was energy hoarded in their odd shapes but they were without aggression and always glided peacefully back into their places, like zoo animals made placid by years of confinement.

When his illness was at its worst, he fancied he saw a magnificent white cat sitting on the ledge outside his hospital window, several floors above the street. The specter was so real that his fingers clawed painfully at the sheet in an effort to reach his bell to call a nurse to rescue the cat who sat so precariously. And in his throat, behind his useless, tightened voice, he formed the words: I want the cat.

But the cat required no assistance. She—for he understood at once it was female—raised one forepaw, not extending her claws, and laid it gently against the glass. By this simple manipulation, she created an opening and entered the room, bringing with her a splendid sense of joy. He felt ripples of excitement rise along his aching shoulders and back, cool, prickly pleasure moving over the areas of pain and tightness. On the inner window ledge, the cat paused and sat back on her haunches. Amos wanted to laugh, knowing that something very clever was about to happen. Then the cat lifted one paw, licked it delicately, and smoothed it across her chest. It was the most sensuous gesture Amos had ever seen, and above the heat of illness he felt a pleasant flush through his body. Without looking directly at him, the cat immediately engaged him as a full partner in her undertaking. She leaped soundlessly from the ledge to the back of a chair, landing with perfect balance on a spot he knew she had chosen in advance. It was an act of such impish artistry that Amos tried to laugh. He sought to catch her eye, to will her to come to him, but her arch gaze, surveying the room now in a slow, measured sweep, told him that she was in charge, would move only at her own bidding. And this, too, Amos found delightful. It allowed him to slip into restful observation, released from responsibility.

The cat slipped to the floor and arched her back as if reliving some delectable memory of arduous interchange, challenge met and overcome, a gesture of both defiance and mastery that elicited a deep wine-flavored response from Amos's body, as if he too were reveling in the memory of the act along with the cat.

Time was suspended, act and thought merged. He raised dim eyes from the cat and sensed sudden omnipotence in his body, as if he had only to raise his hand to sweep aside the wispy clouds that hung motionless beyond his window, to set the pale, aseptic walls of the hospital room undulating in sensuous waves, to send rainbows spinning out from his fingertips like spiders' webs to fill all of the room with patterned color and light, creating some harmonious three-dimensional design that had never before existed.

From this hallucination, he slipped into sleep with a joy so profound it was still present when he half woke, seized by a murderous convulsion. When drugs had mercifully calmed him, it seemed to him he was now entering a dark, many-tunneled cavern in search of the white cat. He sensed that Noreen had been here just before him. Some pleasant scent of her presence, a floral fragrance, hung in this rough-hewn, stony place. Then, while joy still drew him forward, he discovered that his body was carrying him backward. He attempted to raise his hands and found them locked tightly to his sides, as if he were tethered by ropes. He felt himself sucked from the cavern and set spinning in a vast, neutral space. Then a harsh wind rose and propelled him through kaleidoscopic colors. A chorus of buzzes from armies of insects rose in his ears, became a lament, and he found himself engulfed by sadness. He began to weep, and then to sob frantically, for he saw it was his own will causing him to withdraw. The sullen wind deposited him roughly on cold, moist earth, and he saw above him the slowly-turning wheel of his bicycle.

In the fourth week of his illness, lucidity returned. His doctors ruled that his recovery was assured, a small miracle. The stiff grip of pain released his tortured body. Vito came to visit, a large lump of grief and remorse. Amos took the hand extended to him in both of his own. Hunched beside the bed, his friend looked like a huge, disappointed puppy. "Vito, Vito," Amos chided, unable to control his amusement. Vito blinked, then seemed to understand he had become the butt of some joke. With gratitude, he smiled and then began to laugh. It was at this moment Amos realized he was completely sane. He could not recall when he had first understood this fact, but at some point during his illness, the terror had been spent. Many doors had opened and closed. As Vito sat by the bed, Amos's mother came forward and laid her hands on her son's head, then his shoulders and arms, feeling for fever, as if assuring herself he was not altered in any way.

When I Was Married

T he first morning sound I hear is the crash of water in the bathroom sink. It is my mother in a short blue nightgown washing her face in a spray of splashing water. Lying in the narrow bed I slept in as a little girl, a slender stripe of sun edging the north window and falling across the dressing table that is still scarred from my first nail polish, I can see my mother beyond the wall. At fifty-two her skin is smooth, her stomach flat. She does not need the expensive girdle she will pull on under her slim skirt. She splashes water recklessly.

Loretta will wipe up my mother's splashes, as she has for seventeen years. She will cut my mother's grapefruit and pour her coffee. After my mother has left for her office, Loretta will run cool water into the same bathroom sink and wash my mother's blouses and lingerie in mild soap flakes. Although Loretta is sixty-eight, she is still called our hired girl. We are old-fashioned people in an old-fashioned town. I consider these things and I am neither happy nor sad.

When I lived in the tiny apartment on Walnut Street with my husband (my former husband, my ex-husband—it is only four months and I stumble over this language), I learned to do without Loretta, to wash my face without splashing, to set the butter out of the refrigerator ahead of time, and to make the eggs and toast come out together. I took my clothes—*our* clothes—to the laundromat. This language of divorce is very difficult for me.

It is not difficult for my mother. She was divorced when I was two. Sometimes she says *my husband,* referring to my father. Sometimes she says *my former husband,* sometimes merely *when I was married.* Something in her head tells her which phrase is appropriate and her words are always exactly right. The conversation flows on smoothly without interruption. No heads turn, no eyes are averted. This is a skill I must learn now, like bookkeeping. I learn a little each day.

I watch my mother with keen objectivity. Until now I have not seen her as a divorced woman. She has always been simply my mother. I am amazed. All of these years she has possessed knowledge I was not aware of. It is a box I never opened. "Don't model your life after mine!" she pleads with me these days. "I am no example for anyone." Her words take all of her successful years, crumple them like a ball of paper, and throw them away, for my sake. I observe this as a chemist observes a scientific experiment. I will not pattern my life after hers; our circumstances are really quite different. For one thing, I do not have a child. But I watch her.

My divorce was not my mother's fault. I am very clear on this point. My mother is less certain. She will assume responsibility for any mishap that befalls me, a reflex action. Sometimes now she looks at me silently, raising her eyebrows, inviting me to accuse her. Sometimes she treats me as if I carried some terminal illness within my body. If I am sad, she is sad. If I laugh, she laughs, eager to follow along any course that pleases me.

Her name is Nadine. It is an old-fashioned name, not at all stylish, but my mother does not know this, or she does not care. *Nadine.* When she hears her name, she turns with an open, eager expression, a face always ready to smile. I think it is the same expression she had as a tiny child when her papa, my grandfather, called to her across the rooms of the old house in Indianapolis. "Nadine! Nadine! Come, pretty love! Come, sweetest thing!"

She is editor of a newspaper, the *Commercial Enterprise.* Like my mother, the newspaper has an old-fashioned name. It has been published continuously since before the Civil War. The paper has a tradition as the finest small newspaper in Indiana, but my mother is not awed by traditions. Her mind is filled with other things. In a little while she will sit down at her desk, hesitate only a moment, and then begin to write. She will write about the state highway commission's decision, perhaps she will write about the man who has filed for the vacant position on the school board. She does not like him. A man in public life has a difficult time in our small city if my mother does not like him, but she is usually fair. I know of no one more fair than my mother.

She will write her piece in longhand because she has never learned to type. When people suggest she learn typing, she raises her hand in an amusing little gesture and brushes aside the idea. She is a very self-confident person (except just now, about me).

She comes now, dressed for work, and sits on the foot of my bed, bringing her busy world of ringing phones and committee meetings with her. It is like a mist of scent surrounding her. It hangs in her pale, faintly-pink hair that is colored back near the shade it was twenty-five years ago. Her youthful face with its light scattering of freckles is vivacious. She is telling me about the summer cottage she and Ross Hendrickson will buy.

Ross has been my mother's lover for many years. He is county treasurer. Before that, he was county assessor. When I was a little girl, Ross brought me pencils and notepads printed with the legend, *Office of the County Assessor.* I was not supposed to know that Ross was my mother's lover, but I seem always to have known.

Then when I was seventeen, I came into her bedroom one morning as she was dressing. She was standing before her closet in panties and bra. There was a long red mark across her thigh and she saw me looking at it. "Ross's ring scratched me," she said matter-of-factly, giving me permission to know.

It is my mother who will pay for the summer cottage. She does not tell me this but I understand. Ross is a weak man, a gambler. Once he was accused of fraud, of collusion with a contractor. My mother defended him and the matter was disposed of quietly.

She is comfortable with Ross and his shortcomings do not annoy her. She does not wish to marry him, nor anyone.

When he comes to this house, Ross sits in the large, gray chair and smokes his pipe. His hair is gray now, like the chair, and the firm, flat stomach I remember from years ago pushes out into a little paunch when he settles back and crosses his legs. Ross is quite tall and rather elegant looking. He is handsome in the suits my mother selects for him.

Loretta brings him cake, and tea with a little lemon. She slices the lemon very thin, removes the seeds, and drops two slices into the cup to float on the tea. Ross smiles at Loretta and accepts his cake and tea. He removes his pipe from his mouth and my mother fetches him a little ceramic dish to hold it.

Now, sitting on the foot of my bed, my mother is telling me about a man named Greg, twenty-seven years old, exactly my age, who has just moved back to town from Denver. He is the new assistant manager for the telephone company. I knew him in high school. I remember his round, white face, like a china plate. Greg is not married.

My mother's hands make a picture of him. She speaks carefully, smiling, selecting what she will and will not say about him. She describes him as if he were a candidate she is grooming for office. And everything she says is true.

My mother wants me to be happy; there is nothing she wants more. She tells me I must go out. "There has to be a first time. After that it will be easier." She smiles cheerfully, showing me how easy it will be.

I tell her I must dress for work. I cannot loll in this little girl's bed, I am no longer a little girl.

I am secretary to two lawyers. Like my mother, I do my work very well. The men I work for are quite old, they are fatherly. The eldest is seventy-two. He knew my grandfather who practiced law in Indianapolis. He calls my mother Nadine-girl and kisses her lightly on the cheek when they meet. I have always called him Uncle Jess, since I was a little girl.

If I did my work poorly, I would not be fired. "Don't rush," my employers tell me, but my work is always done on time and they are pleased. They thank me with old men's chuckles and naughtily buy me nightgowns and French perfume at Christmas.

Uncle Jess handled my divorce, treating it, as much as possible, like a skinned knee or a scraped elbow, sitting at his big oak desk writing, comforting me with small, reassuring murmurs.

He has a white moustache that is full and sweeps out to the sides in a very old-fashioned style. The skin of his face is pink and very fragile, old man's skin from which all vigor has faded. His hands are knotted with arthritis. Watching him make my divorce a reality (bringing it to birth, delivering me of this strange burden), I was embarrassed. It did not seem a proper matter to put into these gentle hands. I was sorry I had troubled a kindly old man with this absurdity.

As he sat writing, creating my divorce as if it were a land deed or a traffic ordinance, I looked away and wished I had gone to Nevada. I wished for some impersonal, hardened, faceless clerk who talked in a bored monotone and processed papers as automatically as a computer processes numbers.

Looking past Uncle Jess through the window and down at the traffic moving up Meridian Street, it seemed to me that divorce was a province of the young, like bikinis, motorcycles, and rock music. Not a thing to flaunt before one's elders. Divorce is composed of harsh voices and accusations, cruel and petty acts, childishness. I charged myself with all of this wickedness and sat before him in hot, uncomfortable silence.

How arrogant I had been to put this ugly burden on Uncle Jess!

He belonged on his farm, standing beside his beautiful bay trotter, patting her and chatting with his caretaker, running his hand over the smooth shafts of the sulky and talking earnestly about the races at the county fair. He belonged in the large, graceful dining room of the Adler Hotel, sipping bourbon in five o'clock ease and rising to greet my mother with a courtly kiss.

Then on the day before we were to appear in court, Uncle Jess stopped writing and spoke to me. I looked into his face and saw cold steel in the usually mild blue eyes. The familiar voice changed as he warned me of the possibility of unpleasantness, as he instructed me. I was astonished. This man was an authority on wickedness! Why had I not known this? It was completely logical. In my mind, then, I saw him walking into court with women who were to be divorced—yesterday, twenty years ago, the years before I was born. I had worked beside him every day and I had never before seen this side of his character. It was as if he had suddenly shown me an obscene picture. I was shaken. I know things now I did not know before.

My mother has a little scrapbook I made when I was in fourth grade. It is titled: "The Things I Know About Good Health." I could make a similar booklet now: "The Things I Know About Divorce."

I rise from my little girl's bed, press my mother's hand, assuring her, agreeing, wanting suddenly to please her. I go and stand in the shower; briefly, I cry, but only briefly. I dress swiftly, a pale yellow suit trimmed in white eyelet, a coil of white beads, the butterfly earrings with their tiny diamond eyes. Yellow is my best color. I push this thought aside, I do not let it enter my mind.

Later, sitting at my desk, my work becomes automatic and I find myself talking silently to an imaginary man. He has no face. I am telling this man I do not wish to marry. I say the silent words lightly, making small, imaginary gestures like my mother makes, phrasing and rephrasing the imperfect words. I do not know what this man expects of me and even in my imagination my gestures are awkward, my face a stiff, uncomfortable smile. I ask myself if I *do* want to marry again and the question hangs in the air like a puff of smoke on a windless day.

I try to recall the boy from high school and I vaguely see a young figure in a wrinkled gym suit shuffling across the tennis court, flipping his hair from his perspiring face and drinking at the water fountain.

At five o'clock, I close my desk and walk down the stairs of this old building with its high ceilings and ornamented woodwork. When I was a child, our dentist's office was on the second floor and the stairway was a dark tunnel of dull brown. Now everything has been repainted in light, misty green. The wooden handrail has been replaced by a slender aluminum rod. The worn stairs have been refurbished with a bright covering.

On the street, I turn and pass the drugstore where children still come after school to buy soft drinks and thick pretzels from a glass jar on the counter. I catch sight of my reflection in the long window and note, with a little surprise, that I look like pictures I have seen of my father.

I glance at my watch—it is only thirteen minutes past five—and pause to look at the display in the window of the jewelry store. Silver music boxes set with pale blue stones sit in a half-circle on a dark velvet shelf, like a miniature orchestra ready to perform.

At seventeen minutes past five, I pass through the door of the Adler Hotel and walk across the soft, rose carpeting to the dining room. From a table near a window, my mother's hand lifts in cheery salute and Ross, genial, a bit fatherly, gets to his feet. A young man a little shorter than Ross, with a tanned face nearly hidden by a blonde beard, rises beside him. I pause and the face above the beard becomes familiar. It is

131

older, a man's face now. As I cross the room and take this man's hand, I discover I can smile.

I am grateful to the waiter bringing drinks, for a basket of crackers to pass, for my mother's easy chatter. But I know, finally, that I must speak. "What did you do in Denver, Greg?" I venture at last. My voice sounds ridiculous.

"I skied," he replies and grins, knowing he is equally foolish. The grin makes lines around his eyes and ties together all the parts of his pleasant face. He begins to talk about skiing; my mother and Ross nod and comment. The three voices are a soft, textured web of sound that asks nothing, expects nothing, and I hear beyond the words some orderly process at work, creating a pattern that will carry the events of this hour into the next, and the next after that. It is a stitchery of voices repairing one day and creating the next.

"Have you ever been to Colorado?" Greg asks me.

"Yes," I reply and hesitate, but only for a moment. "I was there once, when I was married."

Greg nods, Ross draws on his pipe, a waiter appears and my mother greets him by name. The hum of voices resumes, drifts out from the table and across the room to merge with other voices, neither louder nor softer than before.

The Bengal Tiger

I don't think I really believed Harvey when he said he was going to buy a place in the country and raise foxes. "Red foxes, Catherine," he said, pulling his fat cheeks back into a large, pompous grin so that he looked a little like an oversized child, a little like an evil cat. But you could not disbelieve Harvey. He was unpredictable. Capable of bizarre, audacious acts, he was also often filled with empty talk. The two qualities created a sense of uncertainty about him and made him just a little sinister, a fact he understood and cultivated. He considered it his best point and saw himself, in a rather ridiculous way, as an adventurer.

Before he moved to the country he used to stop by and have coffee with us on his way to work in the morning, coming up the drive in the red Lincoln and waving to Bunny and Karl who would be waiting for the school bus at the corner. He would walk into the kitchen, a sturdy barrel of a man above six feet, in a business suit and western boots, thirty-five years old and still looking to me like my husband Clayton's baby brother. "Good morning, Catherine," he would say, solemn as a parson, like someone burdened with heavy duties, the soft mouth sucked into a thin, straight line, the black hair on his huge head dressed with some odorous cosmetic. Harvey does not look much like Clayton except that they both have Mother Harmon's black eyes, and when you see how Clayton's hairline has crept back you can see how Harvey will look in five years. He has never married.

I would pour out a large mug of coffee for him, made with chicory, the kind we always had at home. I don't think you can get it in any restaurant here in Milwaukee and that was partly why he came. Then I would tell him Clayton wasn't up yet, like a ritual, and we would talk, Harvey trying to drink the steaming coffee with delicate little movements, the gold ring set with the opal from Mother Harmon's brooch clicking against the cup. Mostly he would talk about his job, how some diode or tuning coil worked, and I would follow along minute to minute, and then lose it as soon as he had finished what he was saying. Harvey fooled a lot of people with his sideshow manner and his Southern accent, but he has two degrees in engineering, the same as Clayton. Clayton and I have lost most of our accent. Colored people do not draw back from us as they sometimes do from Harvey.

In the warm kitchen, in the morning disorder of crumbs and plates, he often called me "sister" in the Southern manner, and although the talk was usually light, sometimes he brought up old topics. He would recall some childhood memory and relate it as if it had special meaning and were somehow a little dangerous. With his foolish intensity he managed to create a sense of conspiracy that was slightly unpleasant.

"Harvey," I said to him once, exasperated, "everyone at home is dead. There's nothing left but the cemetery. Let it alone."

He smiled—the slightest hint of contention stimulated him—and launched a fantastic defense. "I've always been a dirt farmer. I still can't sleep past five in the morning. That life shaped me, Sister. I can't change myself into something else. I'll always be a country boy who knows the worth of a dollar."

It was an unsuitable response, and it was untrue. Their father had always had colored to do the farm work, the same as my father, and Harvey and Clayton could have lived out all of their days on the money Mother Harmon left them. But Harvey could never let things be as they were. He would take

134

what was there and add something that wasn't there, even when he was small. When he was seven years old he would conjure a witch woman in the woodpile and make it so real that all of us, the five or six children who played together, would be shivering with fear, and someone would go running off to Mother Harmon to tell on Harvey. And afterward he would not admit it hadn't been real. Even when Clayton and the other boys dragged him behind the shed and whipped him, Harvey would stand there swearing his witch woman had been real and he could bring her back any time he chose. He'd stand toe to toe to the bigger boys, never struggling to get away, until they turned him loose. Then he would walk off, jaunty as a cock, showing who had won. And I would be the one who went after him, five years older and all little mother, to make him a hollyhock doll or peel an orange for him, set on taming him out of his mischief.

And so one morning it was foxes. He had just returned from Europe where he had been directing the installation of microwave relay towers. Traveling by train from Lyon to Geneva he had seen, or fancied he'd seen, a red fox standing in the snow on the side of a mountain. "He stood so still he could have been a statue," he said, "or an odd formation of tree branch resembling a fox, except for his eyes. His eyes were bright and alive, and he looked directly at me, straight into my eyes. I wanted to leap out of the train and catch him in my hands!"

The thought of Harvey, nearly three hundred pounds of him, leaping from a train and scampering up a mountainside after a fox made me laugh helplessly. He looked pained and misunderstood, but he liked feeling misunderstood and sat for a moment, savoring it. Then Clayton came in, holding a tissue to his neck where he had cut himself shaving, and trying to pour out his coffee with one hand, pale with sleep and looking frail, as he always does beside his brother. As tall as Harvey, Clayton is slender and angular with short, graying hair. He is as modest as Harvey is bold.

Harvey recovered immediately. "Clayton, I'm going to buy a little place in the country and raise foxes," he said, making the words a challenge. When Clayton did not answer Harvey began to laugh, taking charge of the silence.

Clayton sat down at the table, daubed at his neck, inspected the tissue, and tossed it into the wastebasket. Then he measured half a spoonful of sugar into his coffee and stirred it. "Why would you do a senseless thing like that?" he said at last, patient and put upon, not looking at his brother.

Harvey threw back his head and laughed louder, as if Clayton had said something nice to him, as if he were swimming in a sea of praise. Harvey was capable of arousing every ugly instinct in Clayton, who was usually the gentlest of men, and Clayton, once his anger had surfaced, seemed incapable of handling it. It put him at Harvey's mercy. It was a trap his brother set for him again and again.

"Harvey," I asked, trying to pull the conversation into some reasonable context, "why do you want to raise foxes?" He smiled, enormously pleased, and turned secretive. "It could be for the fur," he said, "or for medical research, or perhaps for animal food." He counted out these possibilities on his fingers and turned his ring thoughtfully. He was the possessor of some delicious mystery that he was not yet ready to share with us. He watched Clayton's growing irritation with amusement.

"Well," I said to Clayton, trying to help him "when he decides, I'm sure we'll be the first to know." But Clayton ignored me and my contempt was lost on Harvey. Some message had passed between them.

Clayton made a noise in the back of his throat, cruel and cutting. "You are all the family I have left," he said. "I have tried my best to keep you out of trouble, but I don't see much point in wasting any more of my time."

Harvey looked directly at Clayton and a flicker of uncertainty crossed his eyes. In another second it was gone but its meaning had been unmistakable. In some obtuse, wrongheaded way, Harvey wanted to please Clayton. He was still a younger brother seeking Clayton's approval. It was sad, and a little frightening.

If Clayton saw it, he rejected it. He was beyond understanding. He addressed Harvey in a cold, controlled voice. "If you want to throw your money around and make a fool of yourself, it is nothing to me. You can have ten red Lincolns and a truckload of cowboy boots for all I care. Buy yourself a fox farm. Buy yourself a Bengal tiger!"

Harvey's fingers gripped the coffee mug for a moment and then released it. "Now that's just what I think too," he said quietly. Then he stood up. "Good morning, Clayton. Good morning, Sister." And he walked out, no faster than he had walked in, not stamping his boots nor slamming the door.

He bought ten acres of land in a neighboring county, five acres of level oak woods in front and five acres of rocky hills and scrub timber in back. There was a nice pond fed by springs, and a fringe of tall pines facing the road and running up the property line on either side. Some previous owner had meticulously planted seedlings, perhaps for privacy, the first step in some careful master plan, and then abandoned the project.

After a time, Harvey began to come again in the morning and now he brought charts and drawings with him and talked about elevation, drainage, and topography. Clayton regarded him coldly or ignored him.

Then he came with the first drawing for the fox pens and spread it out on the kitchen table. Clayton glanced at the smudged paper crawling with Harvey's almost illegible script, studied it for a moment, and finally could not tolerate it. He pulled the drawing to him, took a pencil, and began to make small alterations. That night he said to me, "The basic point is that Harvey has invested in real estate. Foxes are harmless enough, and one thing leads to another. Perhaps in a year he'll marry and build a house." Then he began a new drawing for the fox pens. "Harvey is a good engineer," he said, as much to himself as to me, "but he can't be bothered with details. He is essentially a theorist."

It seemed a curious word.

Clayton put the water pipes down farther below the frost level and added wind baffles on the north. He ordered expanded polystyrene insulation for the walls and roofs and upgraded everything in the bill of materials.

When Harvey saw the drawing he was delighted. "You're spending so damned much of my money I may turn the foxes out and move in myself!" Then he told us about Odell Palmer. "Avery Palmer's grandson." Avery was a colored man who had worked many years on the Harmon farm. "Odell is twenty-two. He wants to come North and go to school, to study agriculture, I guess. He'll need a place to live and I can use someone to help out, so he's going to stay with me."

"What will you live in?" Clayton asked.

"A housetrailer. I'm giving up my apartment. The trailer is being delivered next week."

"Harvey," I asked, "how did you find out about Odell Palmer?"

"He telephoned me."

I could not picture it, Avery Palmer's grandson calling Harvey Harmon for help. But as soon as the trailer was in place, Harvey sent a plane ticket to Odell and asked me to meet him at the airport.

Odell was an astonishing young man. Coming along the concourse in jeans, carrying a knapsack, a violin, and half a package of cookies, he was an anonymous black youth, but when he was closer I saw the Palmer face, the flat cheeks and high brow.

He was cordial and remote by turns. His head was filled with flashes of brilliance and large, gray areas of uncertainty. He began almost at once to talk about Eugene Fodor. In the car and over lunch at home, he spoke alternately of Fodor and himself. He told me he had already completed a bachelor's degree and had come North to audition for a master's

138

class at the university, and to do graduate work. He knew nothing about agriculture. His field was music and his instrument the violin. "But I belong to the popular culture," he said, sitting in our kitchen drinking the chicory coffee and chain-smoking cigarettes. "I belong to cheap shoes and second-day bread. I can never be an elitist of any sort. This is the mentality I bring to things."

All of his opinions were laced with this sort of adolescent bravado in reverse. It made his cleverness, initially at least, very appealing. I liked Odell. I always liked him, even after tensions began to mount. "But you want a concert career," I said. "You admire Fodor."

He had invited the remark but now he looked at me with something like amazement. "Me?" It was wonderfully dramatic, as if I had deliberately embarrassed him. "How is a poor colored boy supposed to key himself into a system like that?" Odell was adept at creating awkward situations.

I felt I should talk to him about Harvey. "I don't know what he's told you," I said, probing gently, "but I think you should know that he is sometimes a difficult man. If you have any trouble, I want you to understand that you can come and stay with us. I want you to promise me that you'll pick up the phone and call if there's any difficulty."

Odell considered, measuring and assessing my loyalties, and decided to confide in me. "Harvey's beautiful!" he said, laughing suddenly. "Mrs. Harmon, he is so beautiful. He is totally unselfconscious. He wants to create a little world just like the world he lived in as a child, and I don't think he is even aware of what he is doing. He wants it all, even down to having a black boy on the place. That's what it is. He's just calling it by a different name. I'm not afraid of him, Mrs. Harmon. I envy him."

"I think you're underestimating Harvey."

"No, I'm right. Harvey cannot corrupt me. I've already been corrupted. I have too much self-awareness. Harvey can plunge into things and let them work their magic on him. I'm always standing off at one side, watching myself. And so I always come out by the same door."

These speeches were elegant. Later, when I heard how well Odell played, it seemed to me that his music and his conversation had something in common, a brilliance that transcended ordinary meaning. And he was a fine showman as well. "You seem to know Harvey quite well," I said.

"He came down to see me twice." Odell saw that I was surprised and laughed. "Did you think he ordered me by phone the way he did the foxes?"

"I really didn't know. Odell, what is he going to do with the foxes?"

"Tame them."

"Tame them?"

"That's it. He's going to take the pups away from the mother as soon as they're born, so they have contact only with humans."

"That's bizarre."

Odell didn't agree. "I've seen stranger things done. I had a part-time job at the zoo at home for six years. I've had quite a bit of experience with animals. That's another reason Harvey wanted me. Nothing about this project happened by chance, you know. Harvey only wants it to seem that way." Odell chattered on. He had dinner with us and left afterward with Harvey in the red Lincoln.

When the contractor began the construction of the fox pens, neither Harvey nor Clayton could stay away. They both left work to supervise, and I had to drive out and take Odell to and from school, since he refused to drive Harvey's car.

He had been accepted at the university with enthusiasm and he was alternately appalled and frightened. He was practicing four and five hours a day and attempting to learn everything at once. Each time he came upon a detail he hadn't known, he was terrified. Finding material already familiar to him filled him with contempt. Harvey, locked into his own thoughts, seemed hardly to notice him. While Odell stood at one end of the trailer practicing scales, Harvey sat at the other, dreaming of his foxes.

The daily rides to school became difficult. Odell was often irritable. "I'm sick and tired of hearing about the melancholy in Tchaikovsky," he said to me one morning, "as if it were something he breathed in with the Russian air. All art is calculated or it isn't art at all." There was more, a great deal more. "I know I'm right," he said, "but how in hell can I say a thing like that?"

But he did say it, one day in class in a burst of frustration. He emerged with a reputation as a gifted analyst. But his triumph immediately soured into cynicism. "Analyst, shit!" he said on the drive home.

"This is exactly what you wanted," I said to him. "You've keyed yourself into the system. Why doesn't it satisfy you?"

"Because it's all a game, just the way it was at home. Next year there'll be another black boy and he'll tell them Tchaikovsky is about faith healing, or maybe universal suffrage."

Harvey and Clayton were as elated as Odell was downcast. They spent all of their spare time in the country. They made sketches, argued, shouted, laughed. They examined welds, puttied nail holes, ate bologna sandwiches. One evening in a frenzy of joy, they threw Odell into the pond.

Harvey became obsessed with the idea that the foxes, which had not yet arrived, were of great value. He had his entire property enclosed with cyclone fencing. He bought a rifle and carried it in the trunk of the Lincoln.

The fox pens looked like dog kennels, four low, square houses set on cement, each separately enclosed. There was an automatic watering system, a storage area for food, straw for bedding. No detail had been neglected. When the pens were ready a pair of red foxes, the female already bred and heavy with life, were installed. They prowled their separate pens with suspicious cunning, their small, hard, angular faces always seeming to smile. They were taut springs of anger eager to explode. Harvey and Clayton tended them so carefully there was little left for Odell to do. It made an incongruous scene: two apprehensive foxes, two childlike men, and strains of the Mendelssohn Concerto floating out from the back bedroom of the trailer.

One of Odell's faculty advisors was a professor named Baron, whom we knew from newspaper accounts. It was never entirely clear how Baron, a member of the social science department, had become an advisor for Odell who was enrolled in the school of fine arts. Baron had initiated the relationship. He had marched with Father Groppi in the open-housing demonstrations of the sixties, over the Industrial Valley Bridge and into the South Side where he had been struck in the face with a rock thrown by a spectator. The wound had left a deep, ugly scar under one eye. As we waited for the foxes to be born, Odell talked more and more of Professor Baron. "He has had to rebuild his entire life around that scar." Odell had a car now, provided by Baron through some manipulation of grant money. Baron also took him to lunch almost daily. Now it was Odell who stopped by our house nearly every morning for the chicory coffee. "Everybody else has gone on to other things," he said. "Groppi got married. He's driving a bus now. But that scar won't budge. It's like going to work every day in clothes that are out of style. So now he has me to dandle on his knee. I see right through him and he knows it. He loves it! Being unmasked is some kind of penance for him."

"You haven't an ounce of compassion in you, Odell," I said, "not for yourself nor for anyone else." I felt sympathy for Baron. I was certain Odell was telling him similar unflattering things about us.

Odell seemed to thrive on my motherly concern. Perhaps he believed I accepted his statements at face value. "Mrs. Harmon," he said, "Baron has an Eastern accent. Otherwise he's no different than the professors I had at home. Harvey's a better man any day. He looks at me and he sees a colored boy

142

working on Harmon land. That's something good and solid. You can count on it, like the sun rising. It's about the only honesty I've seen around here."

I felt a sharp retort building, but these self-dramatizing speeches were clearly designed to provoke reaction. I reminded myself that Odell was only twenty-two.

A few mornings later he brought the news that four young foxes had been born. "You should have seen Harvey go in after those pups!" he said, laughing. "In his pajamas! The mother fox was set to kill him. Then he put her in another pen and she just crawled off and whined."

A bit later Clayton and I drove out to see the foxes. Harvey was still sitting in the pen in his pajamas, an ugly gash on one arm but otherwise no worse for his encounter with the mother fox. He was jubilant. He trembled with tenderness. I made scrambled eggs in the trailer and Clayton, as a final precaution, hammered together wooden baffles to completely enclose the two adult foxes in the farthest pen.

On the second day, one of the pups died but the others looked better. Gradually, they began to take the milk mixture Harvey devised for them. Confined in the farthest pen in almost total darkness, the adult foxes grew sluggish. Their fur lost its gleam and they roused themselves only occasionally to take a little water.

When the pups were a month old, Odell brought George Baron to see them. He was a tall, vigorous man with graying hair and a closed expression. The scar was much worse than I had expected from the newspaper accounts and photographs. Bunny and Karl could not take their eyes from it.

It was Saturday morning. Baron walked about stiffly with his hands thrust into the pockets of an old army jacket. It was plain that Odell had prepared him to hate us. Baron watched Odell constantly for cues, like a fencer prepared to thrust in any direction to protect his protégé. But Odell could not have been more cruel. He was filled with inward smiles and small, mysterious chuckles, leaving Baron to decide for himself what form of Southern white trash we were. Harvey hung over the pups, and even Clayton forgot his customary courtesy in a stir of small chores. I took the children and went home.

I did not go back again until the pups were nearly three months old, and I went only at the urging of Bunny and Karl. Clayton had been going out regularly, sometimes taking the children with him, and they were all eager for me to see the beautiful, tame pups.

I was not especially pleased when Baron was the first person I saw standing by the pens. He seemed more at ease than before, but the children's curiosity about him had not diminished. I tried to keep them away from him. When they had fondled the pups for a few minutes, I sent them into the trailer to play checkers. But Harvey would not let me walk away. "There is no reason we have to leave the world the way we found it," he said, looking triumphant. I felt it was a speech he had been preparing for me for some time.

The pups were elegant, sedate and frisky by turns. They stood serenely and allowed themselves to be stroked. When Harvey touched their noses, they ate bits of food from his hand.

"It's quite remarkable," Clayton said, "the implications."

Even Baron had been drawn in. "Whenever you touch on behavior modification you must measure a gain and a loss." As he talked, the deep scar in his face appeared to move independently of his cheek muscles. It pulled upward and outward with small, unpredictable twitches.

"Nothing's lost," Harvey said, his eyes flashing in the large expanse of face.

To my surprise, Baron smiled. Tentative new alliances had sprung up among the men. "I don't suppose fox hunters would agree," he said mildly.

"That's not the point anyway," said Clayton. "We aren't trying to make any judgment at all. We're only gathering information."

Baron considered. "And trusting that the moral judgment can be a simple reduction of data, like an engineering problem?"

I was slightly repelled by the conversation. I moved away and walked down to the farthest pen to look at the parents.

Odell came up beside me. "They're gone," he said quietly. "It got worse, much worse. Harvey got rid of them."

"I see. So it's come to that. Well, what difference does it make? Harvey has what he wants. They all have what they want. The foxes are tame."

Odell started to say something and seemed to reconsider. I looked at him and saw that his hands were trembling. He took hold of the fence to steady them. "Mrs. Harmon, the foxes aren't just tame. They're blind."

"Odell . . . blind?"

"They don't know it," he said softly. "Harvey and Clayton and Baron. I kept thinking they'd notice."

"Odell, are you quite sure?"

"Mrs. Harmon, I worked in a zoo for years."

I resisted. "You could be wrong."

He shook his head. "I went in and talked to the people in animal physiology at school. They weren't even surprised. They said it happens with wolves all the time. They think there's an enzyme in the mother's milk that's necessary for the final development of the eyes. There's even an eye institute doing research on it."

"And you haven't told anyone else about it at all?"

Odell shook his head again. "No, ma'am."

It took me a moment to recognize his voice, and then I remembered it quite clearly. It was the voice of his grandfather, Avery Palmer. Odell had retreated two generations in a few seconds. I could have been—should have been—considerate of his feelings. I should have turned and walked away, and spoken quietly to Clayton. I should have spoken out the first time Odell annoyed me with his cynicism, pretended or otherwise, before resentment gathered. The anger I now felt was for Harvey, but Odell, like a pesky, buzzing insect, drew my fire. "Why haven't you told them, Odell?" I asked, freezing each word into ice. "It's only a game. Isn't it time you told them it was all a game? March in on both feet, Odell. Draw blood. You find us all terribly amusing, don't you?"

He stepped back as if he had been slapped and I realized what I had done. The moment was so pathetic, so ridiculous, that it did not seem real. It seemed a terrible, tasteless joke. I began to walk and then to run back to the first pen where Clayton was kneeling beside the pups. I seized one of them and passed my hand before the bright, empty eyes. Then I examined the second, and the third. There was a frantic blur of voices, and then absolute silence.

The sun had begun to slant through the tall pines, painting us all into cold shadows. I saw Clayton's fists clench for a moment and then relax. Harvey was first to move. He turned and began walking away, up the little rise toward the pond. Clayton got to his feet and watched his brother for a moment. Then he went to the Lincoln, opened the trunk, and took out the rifle.

It was George Baron, veteran of violence, who took charge. He went into the trailer and came out carrying Bunny, leading Karl by the hand. He put them into our car and lingered a moment until they were settled. Then he turned to me. "Go, Catherine," he said quietly. "Just go."

But I could not leave Odell. He was standing by the fox pens staring away from us and into the woods where the thick brush of forsythia had begun to blossom. I went to him and laid my hand on his arm, but he had regained his composure and it seemed for a moment that he was unwilling to relinquish his distance. Then he turned and looked at me levelly, with just the faintest suggestion of a smile, and I saw it was something much more complicated than composure. He looked refreshed, as if he had just finished a brisk walk or a splendid meal. He slipped away from my touch and took my hand in a neat handshake. "Mrs. Harmon, thank you, for everything."

I saw the same cool, brilliant, professional face again a few months later in the newspaper with the information that he had accepted a post with a symphony orchestra in the East, and once again the following summer when we drove down to Chicago to hear him play Paganini in recital. The following day the critic for the *Tribune*, who had liked the performance, wrote, "Seldom since Ysaye has this music been played with such diabolical splendor. Palmer is fired by machinery as rich and uncompromising as sin itself." Perhaps that is how fine music is made.